Marina

Aoibheann McCann

WORDSONTHESTREET

First published 2018 by

Wordsonthestreet

Six San Antonio Park, Salthill, Galway, Ireland
www.wordsonthestreet.com
publisher@wordsonthestreet.com

A catalogue record for this book is available from the British Library.

ISBN 978-1-907017-49-0

Cover design, layout and typesetting: Wordsonthestreet
Printed and bound in the UK

Marina

About the author

Aoibheann McCann is a widely published writer of fiction, non-fiction and poetry. She features regularly on the Irish literary scene, both as a performer and an MC. She was raised in Inishowen, Co Donegal and currently lives in Galway with her husband, daughter and two dogs. *Marina* is her first novel.

To Anthony and Saoirse

Prologue

I'm bubbling under the water, trying to reach the surface, held down by the sheer weight of it, choking.

'Go with it Marina, give up to it.'

The fear is crushing, even heavier than the weight of the water. I let go and plunge downwards; a last bubble of air escapes and charges to the surface.

I open my eyes.

'What did you see?' he whispers.

I remember green murky shapes; I close my eyes again.

He tells me not to fight, to relax, but the fear overwhelms me, I start to choke. He calls me back.

I rise to the top of my unconscious once more; I squint and rotate my head. Dust plays in the beam of light from the small window above the door.

Still observing, clipboard on knee, he smiles in a patronising fashion.

'Welcome back,' he says lightly, 'You went further this time, we are making progress.'

I turn away and close my eyes again, momentarily back there of my own choosing, suddenly aching for the depth, the envelopment. I feel empty.

He rises to leave when I open my eyes again.

'Same time next week.'

He doesn't ask for my consent, and swishes out of the room.

I have been here for a long time, but not long enough to have left a mark on the room. It is bare and windowless, apart from the one above the door. Painted pale creamy yellow, probably 'Institutional

Yellow' or 'Industrial Cream' on the Dulux colour chart. It achieves its purpose by anaesthetising me back into my semi-conscious state.

I awake longing for Jamie, knowing he is there at the bottom. I must be as brave as he was, as trusting, to reach him.

If a newborn baby is thrown naked into water in the first few months of life, it swims; however, without repetition the ability is quickly lost. Fishermen shun learning to swim as they shun life jackets, because when the time came you'd fight the water, instead of returning, belonging.

Belonging like they did when I saw them, floating in the sea, the green fronds of seaweed caressing their pale skin. They are nibbled gently, caressed by tiny fish who, bit by bit, ingest them, return them, welcome them.

Days go by, the light through the door window fading in and out.

When Doctor O'Hara returns, he asks me about my earlier fascination with global warming. He must have been talking to Mona again this week. She still has not visited, though I know she talks to him, no one else could have planted these questions so firmly into his notebook.

I don't tell him that I welcome it; it accelerates the return to being at one with Jamie, with her. The flooding rising seas are coming to take me back to where I should be.

Once upon a time, the earth won the battle of the elements. She persuaded the sun to work against the water, so the sun shone down and worked to raise the earth above the sea. But the earth was lonely for the creatures beneath and longed for their caress again, so she called them up unto the land. The sea was angry and raged against her, recruiting the wind to his cause.

Look at the human embryo; its development commences undistinguished from the cow or the seahorse. Even the most primitive growth always maintains a part of its original. Always, within every cell and every piece of plastic, there is water, God, life, everything and everyone.

I don't tell O'Hara any of this, and resist his regression attempts this time.

He smiles, in a way I imagine he feels is reassuring, at this barely-woman who has been hospitalised following a tragedy that has broken her brain in two. It does not occur to him that to crack a seed is to render it powerless; it destroys all that is within.

His question should be, 'Marina, tell me, what is the meaning of life?'

I know the answer now. Since the beginning of time men have fought and died to discover the answer. The answer is this: the very essence of their being, the contents of their cups, the essence that surrounds all, the very one thing we cannot do without. This is the answer to what is God, what is the meaning of life, what am I? Water.

Now I know the answer, what is the point in being in this useless appendage designed for short-lived pleasures?

Men think they are closer to water. They watch their own urine as it ebbs and flows. It stops and starts them on their journeys.

Water breaking is the first sign of life.

When I was two I fell off a rock by the shore, I sank to the bottom; it was beautiful then. Not like now, when I try to relive it. Dr. O'Hara is convinced this incident is pivotal to my recovery.

My father jumped in to save me and I struggled against him, not wanting to go back, but I was returned, born again, gasping and choking, retching in the poisonous oxygen.

I cried for days.

I switch my attention back to his scribbling; he notices this, and asks me about my mother. My parents' early demise is his other favourite

9

cure-all. A stale angle, but I decide suddenly to indulge him. I tell him about the zoo.

This is one of my clearest memories of her: my mother in her high heels and expensive bag, lipstick, scraped back hair. I looked at the lion and then looked back at her. I saw the bars around my mother as clearly; she was as miserable and paced more frantically. She could not see the bars of the cage, but her sense of being trapped went all the more deeply for it.

Then I get carried away and I tell him, 'In the beginning was Hippocampus and cells surrounded it, stuck to it, wanting to belong, and the brain was built clamouring for appendages. It explored the land and soon grew bored. But instead of going backwards it was too proud and went forward, growing upright, trying to reach the sun. But the sea will rise again and take it back.'

He smiles, makes a tick on the clipboard and leaves me alone again.

Part 1

Theta Rhythm

1

The first time I met him was at the bottom of the sea.

Any religion or cult will tell you that the highest state of being is just merely being. Not having to bear petty feelings like jealousy or rage, not caring about material things. Well, there we were reproducing (no guilt about overpopulation or unfair consumption of resources) with purpose, eating and *being*, just *being*, in the darkness. Can you imagine how wonderful it was? Surrounded by water, everywhere its pressure, not needing to think beyond swimming around and around.

Seahorses and fish are philosophical creatures. So deeply philosophical that they can look at the same thing again and again and see it all in a million different ways. The object in view can trigger off a million different thoughts.

It was heaven, nirvana, call it what you will. We were the closest I think we veer to that man-made fantasy. We had been together for as far back as my seahorse being was. Maybe we were brother and sister too; it didn't matter then. Our home a rock with a hole in it, to dart in and out of and just *be* until we died. Which we eventually did.

I was re-born kicking and screaming and gulping the strange air. What I had done to deserve this I couldn't comprehend. It was bright beyond imagining, cold and bare and everything the opposite of how it was before. The very air that surrounded me frightened me. It all seemed too loose somehow, like my body could fly apart in any direction. Fly out around this mustard-and-black-flecked box and splatter on these strange creatures. Who promptly washed me. Which made it worse. It was like having my scales scrubbed off. They stuck me in a box while I got acquainted with the strange body and limbs. Which were impossible to control, jerking out all over the place. The noise that seemed to come from me, how awful it was, but I couldn't stop it. I just screamed and secreted endless amounts of fluids, as the other strange creatures looked at me with as much dismay as I felt.

I kept up the screaming, cursing the world for plucking me from the depths of the ocean and pure being into this miserable existence, where I was hot and sticky and puerile and totally unable to fend for myself.

Something was rammed in my mouth every four hours on the dot, a nasty tasting rubber teat that leaked a congealed, milky-white substance. I slept as little as I could, trying to figure out a way to escape this hell and get back to the dark silent bliss of the home I had been plucked from.

The first time I slept, I thought the wheel had reversed its cycle and I was back. When I slept it was like being back there. He was there in my dreams, he who had always been. It was dark and peaceful. Waking up was like dying all over again and being reborn into this unbearable brightness. Then the screaming would begin again, with more intensity and fervour than before.

The hospital was bright. The fluorescent light shone above my cot and was blotted out only by occasional faces. My mother pale and drawn, too old for this birth and out of practice with babies. It had taken as much out of her as it had me. We were kept in for a week. She shuffled to the canteen as much as she could get away with and left the nurses to feed me. They were brisk and routine-like.

'Ah, she's left the afterthought alone again,' they'd say when she was out of earshot.

My mother's short, stiff perm was unmanageable without her twice-weekly blow-dry at the hairdressers. That week at the hospital was the only time she didn't wear make-up that I can remember. I think even my father had forgotten what she really looked like without it, and maintained his distance. Her dressing gown was the only bright thing, cerise pink with flowers appliquéd on the quilting.

14

And the matching slippers, all bought for the stay in the hospital.

She had done well only to have had two children up to now. Maybe she had been hoping for a boy this time, or maybe I was an accident. Either way, she was clearly disappointed when she stared over from the bed.

So were my sisters, though they only came a few times as the hospital was over an hour's drive away. They crowded over me at first, pawing at me, awkwardly picking me up. My screams and rigid body made sure they soon put me down. They sat at the edge of the bed side-by-side, staring, frightened of this ball of fury that did not belong to their little world. They'd stick their tongues out at me and roll their eyes. Maybe they were trying to make me laugh, but I never did. Not then or after.

When my father came he would stand awkwardly at the end of the bed. He was much hairier than them, more animal-like. But he kept his arms folded firmly and did not even try to pick me up. Though he seemed less annoyed by my presence than the others. I think he understood me then. Like me, he just wanted to get out of the hospital.

I hated prams, high chairs, shoes, baby grows and nappies. I fought to escape all the methods of restraint, all the cages that are used on babies. But as the days went by, I became more resigned to my fate, I became somewhat calmer. It got darker and the wind howled, soothing me high on the hill where the house was. I was still determined to do what I could to get back all I had lost. I cried with frustration at this useless human body, which could not swim or even communicate my request that I be thrown back into the sea and left there.

It was like my soul had been gutted from my body, like the poor fish I saw on the draining board of my new home, sliced in two, its insides pulled out, its lifeless eye gazing in despair at the Aertex ceiling. I remembered little about my death so perhaps this had been it, in this very house. Maybe, somehow, the vitamin-rich flesh I had provided for their Catholic Friday fish fry-ups had infected the very ovaries of my mother, and I had seeped in and come out the other end. Nine months later I could imagine I still felt the knife right through my guts.

But as I said, I began to feel more resigned. What could I do but give in? They did not listen to what I was saying. Even if they could, they would not have obeyed.

I looked for other clues, staring out the window at the restless grey sea from my high chair, which I had given into when I realised it was the only vantage point that gave me a glimpse of the sea. It was also preferable to being held up to look at it, by frustrated and bored and despairing family members. Eventually, when they realised this, and only this, would stop the crying, I was left there almost permanently. I was to be found in the sunroom, feeding on the scraps left on the high chair's table.

From there I stared out the window, but instead of figuring out an escape route, I began to forget. I didn't feel like talking; I had nothing to say to these people, and they didn't talk to me much either. I was waiting for it all to make sense. In the waiting came the forgetting that comes to all humans. My old life began to fade, but it left the new life tinged with an aura of grey.

My family met for a feeding frenzy once a day around the Formica table. There was four of them and they pretty much ignored me; if they didn't I'd start crying.

So they talked while I listened and picked up what I could, without fully taking in its content. I had joined the table first in the pram, staring at the ceiling, grizzling as my mother rocked me as she ate, her foot pushing the wheel over and back. I had listened as I stared at the blankness above, inhaling the trapped cooking oil, learning to turn my head and focus on the windows. Sometimes, when my sisters drew love-hearts in the condensation, it allowed me a partial view of the dark sky.

As I learned to sit up, I was put in the high chair. Slumped down into it, my curved spine only suited to water and cradling. I was put beside my mother's place at the bottom of the table. Before I could feed myself, she'd feed me sideways, almost automatically, barely looking as the powdered Milupa mix smeared my face. I opened my mouth to be filled. She turned every once in a while, when she wasn't speaking or eating, to scrape my face and bib with a spoon and then cram those bits in too.

My sisters squabbled amongst themselves, kicking each other under the table. They laughed at my father's descriptions of the local men who worked for him.

Here at the table, I learned the human preoccupation with fears, jealousies, appearances and hate. Hate that oozed from their pores. They were full of disgust for each other and for those who lived in the village surrounds that I could not see. The others they talked about were inadequate: too fat, too hairy, or too stupid. I would try to tune it out with the sound of the sea, or focus inward on the sound of my jaws moving.

I was slow to crawl as I cried when put out of the highchair, and the flat, unyielding surfaces slapped against my soft palms. But I soon sped up in an attempt to get back to the sunroom. I could not see the sea from the floor, but I'd roll onto my back underneath the climbing plants like seaweed across the glass.

I could smell the sea from here. I'd close my eyes and inhale its comfort. But the knife dragged through my soul as the place I yearned for slipped further and further away. As my mind began to fill up with words I lost more of the pictures and sounds and feelings and being and belonging.

It was in the conservatory that I was happiest, apart from when I slept. At night, the undersea world called to me in my dreams like Morse code.

I screamed again for a week when we moved from that seafront home to the mansion of my parents' dreams. However, with the move came Polly, an Old English Sheepdog. My sisters had insisted on the dog from the Dulux paint adverts, then promptly got bored with her. I loved her. We'd roll around in the field next to the house together, and I'd feel less lost in those moments.

Lying in the long grass, we'd stare at the clouds above as they formed into shapes like sea monsters, Titan, mermaids, shells and even submarines. They'd work their way across the blue until they merged to form huge grey whales and the rain would fall around us. Then someone would come and drag us back into the house and fire us into the bath.

2

Once, my mother took me to see a woman in a small room in Dublin. She stared into my eyes and mouth and asked me to fill in pages with colour. Then I had to make sounds as she clicked her fingers at my ears.

I baffled her.

She could not define what she thought was wrong with me, and rebirthing was not in her vocabulary. I often wonder what would have happened if I had landed in with a New Age family who lived in a camper van on the beach; probably there would be no story to tell. My mother seemed disappointed that they had no word to explain my behaviour in public. It may have suited her better to be able to say, 'Sorry, she's autistic,' in whispered tones.

'Sorry, she has had rebirthing trauma and wishes to return to the sea.'

Maybe that would have worked in San Francisco.

That was the same day we went to the zoo and I realised we were nothing but caged animals.

O'Hara asks me about the trip to Dublin again. He must have read my old medical files. I wonder what they say. I wonder what he makes of them. Knowing what he knows now. He says I might have Asperger's, he says I might have Avoidant Personality Disorder.

The specialist did tell my parents to send me to playschool, which they did. My former life was not accepted there. The teacher did appear to listen, but ultimately discouraged such talk. The shock of this world came back again. Oh, the noise and the smells and the cloying food! But the others were like me and told me what they had been: lions, whales, elephants, birds and insects. It was all in how they behaved; you could see it in them.

It was a Montessori playschool. I preferred the boys, who spoke less and were more in touch with their old animal life. They attempted to run, swim and climb as they always had. They would explain to me who they were through elaborate miming and games. The female of the species has always been more willing to blend into the now than the male, hiding their true selves.

Through the Montessori way, we were to be tamed from the wild animals that we were and made human. Montessori was originally intended for slow children in slums, to make them able to button their coats and wash their faces like good, civilised human beings.

I can imagine Maria Montessori, that fine upstanding doctor, scrubbing faces and doing buttons, rubbing all remnants of rebirth and pagan knowledge out of these hungry, malnourished, lonely, new children. Her impatience with these cretins offered up to a white Jesus in the sky. The more she worked with them, the more they forgot what they had been. Playing with long red chunks of wood and large buttons holding together useless bits of cloth on a wooden frame. A fine introduction to the futility of Western capitalist society. The more resigned the children became to their fate as future factory workers, the more Maria was proud of her civilising achievements, which proved her Christian values. She smiled as she advanced these miscreants straight towards a Christian heaven, and put an end to all these strange animal behaviours in between worlds. These slum idiot savants probably lived only barely into their teens. Even with her help they at best ended up breathing their last in a workhouse, after a long day at the button factory.

I began to use simple words, enough to keep the child psychologist off my parents' back, and was left into the playschool every day from 8am to 6pm on the dot. I screamed when I was taken home. At weekends I lay in the grass with Polly.

My fellow prisoners had now forgotten all but a few remnants, and we clung together in our misery like Alzheimer's patients. At least we were together, not with the adults. Even the boys had conformed, slapped into it at home and cajoled into it at Maria Montessori's legacy learning centre. Whatever it took to make us be still and look reasonably content. We were nullified by toxic, brightly-coloured paint, plastic counters and numbing music played over and over. The hypnotic inane rhyming and repetitive lyrics designed to lull us all into this human hamster wheel of existence.

I spent most of the summer at the beach. I'd gaze at the sea, sitting in rock pools, placing my fingers in sea anemones and having my toes rubbed by baby plaice. Here I'd feel whole again, the hole in my chest filled for blissful chunks of time. My family sunbathed, read magazines and made caustic comments about the day-trippers' bikinis.

Sometimes I met other children. We played in silence or pointed innocently at hermit crabs as our intellects and senses began to slow down further, enabling us to talk. Language like a virus, obliterating further my memory of what had been. Seeing and remembering all that was behind us was fading. I copied the other children and spoke in simple sentences haltingly. We spoke them not to each other, there was still no need, but to the adults. I tried out inane, childish statements that were obvious beyond belief. I'd punctuate my games with speech.

'Look at the crab.'

'Dog wants ice-cream.'

'Polly want water.'

'John is my friend.'

My mother and sisters would respond accordingly.

'How cute is that?' their friends would say.

My sisters would roll their eyes, knowing what I was really like, but it soothed them into believing what they wanted to believe. That I was becoming like them.

As the summer went on, it drew us beach children closer to real school. We licked our banana wafers as they dribbled down our wrists and got lulled into euphoric sugar states that would quickly descend into irrational tantrums. Our parents tried to remove the sand from our brightly-coloured nylon bikinis that we had reluctantly accepted unto our beautiful bare skins. More constriction, more loss of sense and premonition.

Back then, when we did bring the dog to the beach, I had to be restrained, as I would fearlessly follow her and wade into the water. It occurred to no one that I should be able to swim, so I screamed to try to convince them. They turned up their radio to tune me out. My sisters were dispatched in turn to firmly haul my small waist back from the waves and place me back in the rock pools at the side of the beach. I'd stick my face into the water and didn't care if I cut my nose on the cream, limpet-encrusted rock. My sobs subsided when the dog returned to bat her paw into the pool from the limited scope of the lead. I was given sweaty cheese sandwiches and a warm 7-up bottle full of crumbs from my sisters' careless seconds. My mother drank tea from a purple tartan flask. Boats would go by close to the shore and I'd look at them in longing. Their coloured sails were free to go where the wind took them. Across the bay and out of sight.

3

Real school began in September.

Most people look back at primary school through a Vaseline-coated lens. So caked in Vaseline that everything is obscured and swimming in its suffocating jelly and the truth about school is drowned in their clogged brains.

Real school was horrendous; I could already read and write. There I was, unable to even stand up without getting permission. '*An-bhfuil-cead-agam-dul-amach*'s only worked if used sparingly. In the cattle pen of forty children the stench was overwhelming. If you've ever been to Montessori or sent a child there you'll know that there's six per group. There were forty children in Junior Infants that year. The noise was combined with the odour of green snot and mingled with chalk dust.

The boys had now entered into deep despair, the final stage before their brain collapsed fully into a civilized state, but they would strike out frequently, in violence against this caging. It is not acceptable for children to be unhappy, for this foggy lens has blocked it out for adults. They do not want to be reminded of the despair that is felt when one cannot even put a civilised logic upon it.

I felt the despair as much as any, but reacted in a different way. The pain it caused me acted like a magnet pulling me to true north. I knew that I must have been put into this valley of tears that we heard about in our prayers for a reason. The prayers came thick and slow: Hail Mary full of grace, pray for us sinners. In the dull, grey, chalky box of a school we howled for what we had lost. We were wrestled down off cupboards and desks. We were asked nicely but firmly to colour-in inane geometrical shapes or the outlines of tractors. We would rub the white pages with dry crayons from plastic boxes. The thick stumps of crayons demanded energy to get even a mark out of them. Our longing for the beach was rubbed away too.

I liked painting; on Fridays I would don an old T-shirt, creating and getting lost in undersea worlds that comforted me. I would press my face into the end result, only to be removed with a sigh by Miss O'Connor, who would always comment on what a wonderful picture it could have been. Once she managed to rescue one before I joined it. It won a competition and ended up featured on the milk cartons. I received a beautiful set of brightly-coloured paints in the post that I was not allowed to use at home. They ended up in a high cupboard I could not reach.

Miss O'Connor was a well-meaning teacher who recognised my artistic talents, even amid all the madness of an overcrowded Irish country school. She was a willowy woman in her early twenties trying to adjust to the life put upon her by her farmer parents, who were seeking a good secure life and pension for their eldest daughter. This permanent job had been clipped out of The Irish Independent classifieds by her mother. Miss O'Connor was struggling in this small village that was eons away from the bright lights of the city. I'm sure she missed the freedom of college life and had only got a sniff of it from the digs, the limited budget of college and every weekend home on the bus. The four-hour journey home, her mother asking her had she met anyone yet. The dullness of her mother's life reflecting Miss O'Connor's own future.

She lived a lonely existence in a snotty sea of children hopping with lice that even hopped on her from time to time, resulting in embarrassing visits to the local chemist. This was a sure way to broadcast their presence and focus the blame on her. The village could not have been her idea of paradise, with nowhere to go in the evenings and no one to talk to about anything that mattered to her. In the staff room the talk of marriage and small children. No one to flirt with in the all-female-bar-the-principal school. Deathly silences interspersed with questions about her past, probing for gossip.

24

There were a few desperate attempts to set her up with their disastrous inbred relatives whom she knew she would succumb to eventually. Helpless as her brain, like all of ours, turned into candy floss. As we ate, slept, and breathed, the wheel turned and the seasons changed.

She brought us through the autumn with rubbed leaves. In winter we made snowflakes, which adorned the inside walls. In spring, we planted sunflower seeds in milk cartons on the windowsills and caught tadpoles in jars. She began to understand why Junior Infants teachers are exempt from jury duty, as they were seen to be unable to make rational decisions given the company they keep all day. Though jury duty would have been a welcome relief.

In the town, she was known as Miss O'Connor; in private she was called Mona. We called her 'teacher' or 'miss', and her identity sank further into the gravel in the school playground. However, she took a shine to me, maybe due to the art competition, or perhaps because of my ability to read. The time allotted for my individual attention was not needed for this task, so could be spent being simply kind. Or maybe she recognised in me the loneliness that she felt: stranded in an alien landscape, scrambling for identity. We both had to make do with blending in as best we could.

I never asked why; maybe I will if she ever visits.

She pandered to my passion for the sea with displays on the wall. Once she even arranged a trip to the beach with parent helpers. The day out turned into a mini disaster, with pupils, unrestrained, running for freedom, and not picking shells as planned.

We were promptly herded back onto the bus in the car park, eating our packed lunches from greaseproof bread wrappers: ham sandwiches and flasks full of very diluted dilutable orange, a stale yellow multipack-bag of cheese-and-onion crisps and a penguin bar, guaranteed to scramble our brains alongside the waft of freedom offered. Miss O'Connor was a nervous wreck in the end, and was glared at patiently by the volunteer mothers. Worse still, the principal looked her at sternly throughout the week left before the holidays. She was never to attempt such a thing again.

Before we broke up for summer, it was she who recommended to my mother that I learn a musical instrument. This must have happened at a parent-teacher meeting. It was my mother who suggested that Miss O'Connor be my tutor for the piano that my father surreptitiously bought in the meantime. My parents told my sisters to pretend to the teacher it had always been there. My mother must have told her we had one at some point during that meeting, or maybe that's what she had told the whole village. Miss O'Connor came once a week on a Thursday throughout the summer, and continued when I returned to school. She was delighted, if embarrassed, to get out of the digs she lived in, and of course had more money to accumulate in the building society. A fund that would never aid her escape, only her capture. Ultimately, the piano lessons only served to radically alter her life, along with my own. The piano was truly the instrument of fate.

I took to the piano although I was a bit young. It drowned out the longing and the grey thoughts in a more pleasant fashion than school. School with its endless workbooks full of tracing and its climbing up and over and up and down the stairs to the tune of the bell to lunch, playground, noise, lice and snots.

So I learned to play under Miss O'Connor, and her benign influence got me through even the worst of my next teacher. Mrs. Ryan was in charge of the Senior Infants. From here she carried out her small-town grudges and prejudices on the children of the people she had gone to school with.

Miss O'Connor began to babysit when my two older sisters went out to distant nightclubs. They'd laugh and iron their clothes, listening to Adam and the Ants, and if I had the misfortune to enter the room they'd dab blue mascara on my brows or on Polly.

'Get out,' they'd then screech in unison.

I was mesmerised by their transformations in the mirrored circles of their dressing table.

'Don't mind them,' Mona would say when I ran back downstairs.

They headed off on old buses, caked in blue eyeliner and boob tubes. With banana combs in their badly permed hair and scowls on their faces as they sneaked past our father, with enough foundation to cover their squeezed spots and a tide line at the chin that would end up on their top later.

My parents went to the golf club at weekends, although they had never played golf in their lives and had no intention of doing so. But my father took off to the Carroll's Irish Open every year, bringing a few local politicians, though they were changing by the month he said. He didn't smoke Carroll's either, he smoked John Player Blues, but they wouldn't be what killed him in the end. I would watch, fascinated, as the smoke swirled from his nose then vaporised into the air, though I hated the smell. My mother's cigarettes were prettier: thin brown Consulate that smelled of mint. These were the ones my sisters stole.

Mona would come over before they all left, and we'd sometimes play with the dog in the garden if it was still light.

'I had a dog too,' she said once. 'He was a boy, his name was Rex, and I loved him.'

'Where is he now? Can he come here to play with us?' I asked.

'Oh Marina, he's gone to heaven with Jesus,' she said, and withdrew to the house before I could ask any more questions.

I suppose I was really her only friend, so inevitably she moved in with us. It made more sense, and so she rented the flat at the back of the double garage, the first in the town. She cooked for herself in our kitchen and that's how she came to meet George Christopher, my mother's gangly cousin from nearby. Our home had been built on my mother's ancestral land. Our home, the two-storey mansion with seven bedrooms and a double garage. The gardens were landscaped on the acre. There was a fountain on the front lawn that was never switched on. I preferred the field next door, with its long grass.

My parents had lived in the States and were heavily influenced by the time they had spent there. They were still referred to as 'The Yanks' before, and even after, their deaths, although they had only lived in America for a few years. My mother had worked as an *au pair* for a rich couple and my father for a builder. When they came home he had promoted himself to sub-contractor. He was away Monday morning until Friday night during the week; he even did occasional bouts in London.

George Christopher came down on occasion to fix things or to put things semi-right. Although he had built it, my father had no time to fix anything in our new house. George C would come and unblock drains, or try to fix the dishwasher.

Mona met George on the concrete outside the back-kitchen window where he stood attaching a black hose to the outside tap, wearing Wellingtons that smelled of cow dung.

They had been courting for over a year by the time I was ready for Holy Communion, white dress and sandals with holy missals on stand-by for full religious married-to-God bliss. Mona came looking for an outfit with my mother and me.

'You look beautiful, Marina,' she said when I came out of the changing room. 'A little angel.'

'I'd rather be a mermaid,' I said, uncomfortable in the dry white netting that scratched my thighs.

She laughed, 'You can be a mermaid at my wedding,' she said. 'I'm going to marry George Christopher.'

I saw my mother roll her eyes in the mirror.

She got me a green silk-style flower girl dress. The inside netting was the same.

I don't know whether it was the monotony of school teaching or the sheer hell of living amongst my family that drove her to it, but she walked down the aisle with George C in a white dress and sandals just like the ones I wore to my Communion.

I married God. She married my mother's cousin George Christopher.

4

George was a nice guy, as guys from the area went, but he stifled Mona, or what she could have been. I was just glad that she would still be nearby. The newly-weds were building their own, more humble dormer bungalow over in the next field. George C was set to take over his father's farm. His father ran a chemical-laden dairy farm of sorts. He drove in arrogant fashion past our house on his tractor with link box. He never waved. His fields surrounded my parents' house and were full of rusty tin baths for the cattle. They had a constant running hose in them whether there were cattle in the field or not. Maybe they stand out in my mind because my older sisters regularly suggested what would happen to me if I did not do their bidding: I'd be made bathe in one of these tin baths.

My head was so full of sin, heaven, infinity and eternity from the First Holy Communion lessons that the lawlessness and lack of morality of the sea was confined to my dreams now. I tried even harder to become like other seven year olds, albeit with my wonderful musical talent. I won competitions up and down the country, much to Mona's delight.

'I dreamed of winning competitions when I was your age, but my father was too busy on the farm to take me.'

'Why didn't your mother take you?' I asked.

She thought about that for a minute. 'Mammy couldn't drive,' she said, 'But she paid for the lessons.'

I pictured her mother as much kinder than mine, but as distant.

There was no doubt that my genius added to my family's social status down at the golf club. I'm sure they took full responsibility for the spotting of my natural talent. I excelled at the piano and got more lost in it accordingly. It masked the wound in my soul that I no longer knew how to heal. I suppose I thought everyone felt the same. Why else were they all so miserable?

I ran home from school every day, as if I was expecting someone or something to be waiting there for me. The postman brought me word not of my past life, but of competitions and piano grade certificates. Somehow I always knew this wasn't what I had been expecting; I was always disappointed after my mother opened the manila envelopes. She'd shout over her shoulder about their contents to my disinterested sisters and to me.

When it happened that she turned her gaze to me, it usually transpired that it was a notice of a *Feis*.

She'd roll her eyes.

'Miss O'Connor has entered you into another competition,' she'd say, in the overly loud and slow voice she reserved for me.

Mona had remained Miss O'Connor despite her marriage, as she would for the rest of her teaching life.

'I suppose we'll have to get you a new outfit though,' she'd say in a brighter tone. That part she liked.

I went to the competitions in dusty old halls in small towns, dressed in a pinafore or a tartan sailor dress, white socks and patent shoes, with my hair in a black ribbon Alice band. Probably looking every bit like Little Lord Fauntleroy's long-lost sister. As I played I sent my longing across the hall to the panel of judges. I scanned the audience as they dutifully clapped. I searched not for their approval, as they thought, but for something else, something that would burst the bubble of tension that I felt.

Then Mona and I would go for a carvery lunch (or Aunty Mona as I called her by then). Wherever the small town, the hotel was on the main street and served the same fare. Yellow soup with floating peas in tin bowls to start. Then lumpy bland mashed potatoes with gravy that scalded my tongue, poured over the stone cold tasteless meat and broccoli or carrots. All boiled beyond redemption. If I ate everything on the plate, it was followed by a lurid yellow and red trifle. Only when my mother came with us was I allowed to order the chicken and chips, which Mona had tried to protect me from. Having no children herself as yet, she was thinking only of what was best in the long run for my health. The greasy, yellow skin of the chicken congealed with the half-cooked pale chips, but was at least broccoli-free.

5

Let me tell you more about my mother, and indeed my father, before they exit the story for good.

Her name was Deborah and his was Jerome. They weren't evil satanic child abusers, and of course, according to the great karmic wheel, it was I who had chosen them in between worlds, for whatever purpose. Maybe it was for their money. It wasn't for love; there was no real affection between us, or, for that matter, between them either.

O'Hara told me I have imposed this on them so as to bear what happened next, but I don't believe that. Of course, it makes sense-but I know it is not true.

My parents were numb in an eighties Catholicised way, repressed by Irish small-town living. In those days, being rich could set you apart from your feelings. Jer numbed himself with work, Debbie with spending. Together they conspired in hiding money from the taxman and weekend drinking at the golf club. Judging by Jerome's red-and-purple-veined bulbous nose, the drinking continued during the lunches with County Council officials and other contractors. I was ten years younger than the older two, Fionnuala and Rachel. They were beyond redemption too, ruined by money and eating too much red meat and too many potatoes. Overall, I was wholly ignored, but that suited me fine.

When my parents both died in a car crash on the way back from the golf course, that even their much-heralded visit to see the pope a few years before couldn't save them from, I honestly wasn't too bothered. This was misinterpreted as shock, but it was the sign I had been waiting for. I knew my life was about to change for the better.

Deborah's mother, my grandmother, had grown up around here. I had never met her, as she died just before I was born. Death and life vying for space. When my parents came back from the States they had got the site from my great uncle, George Christopher's father. Though it had no view of the sea, my grandmother had always wanted to build a house there herself; it had been promised to her by her own father. But my grandfather, her husband, had died young. So she had sent my mother to the States to drum up the money to build.

My grandmother had been going to move with us to the flat in the garage. Though she wasn't the eldest, my mother inherited the family house in lieu of this. They had moved in with her on their return from the States. Fionnuala and Rachel were brought up there; my grandmother was very real to them, though only a photograph to me. Needless to say, there was bad blood among my mother's siblings about her inheriting the house.

My mother barely spoke to her siblings, fights still erupting now and again at funerals and the like. The site had been used for cattle up until they dug the foundations. The Yanks lording it up, my unmarried aunt Mary relegated to a flat in Dublin despite the custom that it should be she that would get the family house. My father had grown up beside my mother; they had known each other all their lives. They were, like everyone in the area, distant relatives on both sides. They had come back to build the house, though they clearly preferred the States. They compared it with everything, from the size of the blocks of ice cream to the cars.

Jerome and Deborah had always dreamed about that house, both of them, every bit as much as my grandmother. George's father, my mother's uncle, spat every time he looked over there, from the day they started putting down the foundations. He screwed up his face and spat, but said nothing. He said nothing about his sister with her strange notions, long dead, whose daughter was building this monstrosity. The site was away from the seashore, as far inland as you could get and still be within the townland. He didn't know why they wanted it.

George's mother liked it; she stared at it when she was washing the dishes, but didn't ever visit while they were alive. Not even when they had the Stations of the Cross. She had been sick that day, she said when asked. I never remember her being sick for the other Stations in the village. She looked down the hill at all the cars parked on the lane. I saw her through the window.

I can picture my mother clearly in that old house, though I was supposed to be too young to remember. She had different cleaning tasks on different days to match her different meals. Lamb chops and potatoes on Monday coincided with the changing of bed-sheets that brought the twin tub out on the kitchen floor. On Fridays, after she had scrubbed the lino on her hands and knees, she made fish and chips in the deep fat fryer.

My father was always busy at work, building the new house or fixing something in the falling down house of my grandmother's. He brought the men down from the site, all of the half-mile, at midday for their dinner. My mother fussed resentfully. My father sat still at mealtimes unless he had a few drinks in him. He was awkward in the world of women.

He was a traditional man and would have loved a son to teach him his trade, let him drive the digger and show him how to smooth the mortar between the breeze blocks of the new house that rose slowly a few miles up the road.

My sisters weren't interested, though they longed for a room of their own; they had a dividing line down the centre of their bedroom in the old house. The line included the walls. They marked out which side they were allowed to put the posters that had come free with *Jackie* magazine. My mother scolded them for untidiness, and poked under their beds with a broom if they tried concealing their teenage mess under there.

My father was the one who had promised them the dog when we moved, as my mother liked to remind him (usually while raging about the hairs it shed from one side of the house to the other). I think he saw the dog as a consolation prize. Instead of a son for him, or a cute placid baby to play with like a doll for the women, they had got me. He had driven all the way down to Portlaoise to get it from the breeders.

My mother used to be paid to mind rich people's children. She had learned from this the importance of appearance over attention. I took great exception to the frilly dresses she dressed me in, they were awkward and starchy. Her jaw would clench as I stiffened into each armhole and locked my elbows. We battled and she won, but I punished her with screaming. And a red face that didn't go with anything. She'd turn up the radio and clean the house, as her mother had before her.

Neighbours would call in with their pre-school kids who'd poke at me, but they'd soon lose interest. My mother would make tea in her mother's rose china teapot and they'd gossip about the outfits at mass or the latest happenings in the parish. My mother would always bring up the latest on the new house and how it was progressing in between any jobs that my father was doing. We'd go there at weekends to see how far the grey concrete had spread out on top of the surrounding countryside over the preceding week.

My mother ordered special taps from the North she'd tell the visitors, as she refilled the kettle. Or she'd tell them of the avocado bathroom suite from down the country. Talking about the new home made her smile. My grandmother had never liked the people in the town land she'd married into, and had made sure my mother knew she was better than them. Though my grandmother had been only brought up half a mile away inland. The locals were my father's people too, but even he conceded they had no sense of style. Mostly fishermen and their wives.

My father missed the view of the sea, though he did not earn his living from it; he'd stop the car and stare out at it, silent in the face of the greyness. After we moved he only went to the old house to fix things for the renters. It's still there, but it's been sold and done up for weekenders. The damp ripped out at last. Even my mother liked to call in unannounced on one errand or another before she died.

'Filthy,' she'd mutter as we left, 'Poor mother would be turning in her grave if she knew.'

I'd listen to see if she was, my face close to the ground, when we went to the graveyard after eleven o'clock mass. My mother would rearrange the green marble chips on the double grave. The chips were first of their kind in the graveyard; my grandmother had chosen them herself before her death.

My parents were buried just down from her in the same row. They got white marble chips, but I never heard them turning either.

6

Mona was eight months pregnant when she moved from the garage into the house officially, though she had been there since my parents' accident. I had awoken that morning to her stricken face. She had knelt down to tell me what had happened in a simplified Catholic way. Baby Jesus had taken my parents to heaven or some such rubbish. I imagined them floating back into the sea, happy at last, reunited with all. I smiled; Mona pretended not to notice.

Though I know she must have told O'Hara about this, as he sees it now as the beginning of all the trouble.

I was very curious about the coffins that stayed in our house for two nights before the funeral. Jerome and Debbie staring out at us, cold and rigid but heavily made-up to disguise the injuries. I liked looking at them, though Mona gently pressed me out of the dining room on several occasions.

'Come on now pet,' she said the first time, bringing me back to the kitchen where she was making sandwiches with George's mother.

But when she found me there for the fourth time she did not speak at all. Just turned me by the shoulders and walked me out, away from the coffins and the photo of them at Knock basilica when the Pope had visited. I went back to the shocked and the crying-especially when they caught sight of me-relatives and neighbours.

A crowd of locals and relatives from further afield had converged on the house. All the local councillors and TDs were there too, though my father's hero, Charles Haughey, did not appear.

There was a bowl of cigarettes on the sideboard. White folded sandwiches lay in a variety of dishes everywhere. Chocolate bars were handed out of every handbag and suit jacket. So when I threw up from pure sugar mania people cried all the more, thinking it was the grief that had caused it. George's mother and my older sisters poured out tea from giant dull aluminium teapots with black handles. I watched as my sisters hugged distant relatives in a daze. Fionnuala had started college in Dublin by then. Rachel was just about to, pending the all-important Leaving Cert results, and would go to college in Dublin too. The lack of career prospects an arts degree would bring was irrelevant. Neither of them would ever have to work due to the size of the life insurance combined with my parents' accumulated wealth.

I don't remember my sisters being around much after the funeral. When they did return they came with French nails and bleached hair, bigger perms and even more foundation. They weren't interested in me or anything else but going to the local nightclubs, chasing local boys. Mona's role was reduced to making up their beds and trying to guilt them into spending time with me.

'Don't mind them,' she'd say.

'They're just teenagers, sure, I was the same.'

I didn't like the thought of that.

7

With death comes life, and what a life it was.

Baby Jamie blazed into my life with bright red hair, and thus came the abrupt end to my wait. Suddenly life was brighter. It was as if I had been living in black and white and was now finally switched to colour. When I try to think back to before he was born my memory is monochrome, with pain dulling its edges.

Everyone was happy that I was happy, now that the hole had been filled. The hole they believed had been blasted by the death of Jerome and Deborah. I knew my parents had been removed as their task had been fulfilled. They had reunited me with Jamie. Of course, I didn't articulate that then. I was too happy. Just as being away from the sea had made me cry, he cried when I was away from him.

We were enraptured with one another. I loved him from the first time George took me to the hospital. The same one I had been born in. I hadn't been back there since, though my parents had spent their dying hours there.

Jamie was red and squashed, as if he'd come out of a shell. Mona showed me how to pick him up gently. He was swaddled in his yellow blankets. I put my nose down against his forehead and breathed him in until Mona's hand pushed me back. I didn't want to put him down again. I didn't want to leave him there, alone and stranded.

I was waiting at the door when George brought them home. I had been in George's mother's, but had run down the hill when I saw the car pulling up. George's mother did not come down. George had to bring Jamie up to her, but she never delighted in him the way I did. George's father took no notice of him at all. Maybe it was because of what happened. Maybe George's mother saw the whole thing floating before us like a tsunami hanging over our heads, waiting to crash down on the house and all of us with it.

I stood by the edge of the pram in a constant vigil. Sticking my index finger down for him to anchor onto. His bright black eyes took me in as they changed to blue. They shone out from his red face with its wisp of red hair. I'd whisper the things I knew, so he'd know it was OK. I told him what was coming, what other people couldn't hear or tried to forget. But we'd face it together; he knew.

So he cried a lot less than I had been remarked to, as now we were together in the same realm again, though he too shuddered in an attempt to breathe the air. This frightened Mona.

'He's fine, he'll get used to it,' I said to Mona.

She smiled at me weakly, 'I hope so,' she said, her eyes bloodshot and glistening.

Still, she went back to work pretty soon after the birth and left a local older woman to mind him, and pretty much me too. I was often at home on one pretext or another. I was miles ahead at school. The other teachers said nothing; they were probably relieved not to have to deal with me. I had never formed a relationship with a teacher after Mona, quite the opposite in fact. Had she not been working at the school, I expect my treatment would have been much more brutal. Instead they had become indifferent, and acted as though I wasn't there at all. My parents' death, of course, was another reason to let my frequent absences go unnoticed in the staffroom.

I had never really made any friends at school, after the initial sympathy bonding with those who attended the local Montessori. After that the children drew away from me. We alienate ourselves from that we wish not to see in ourselves, or that which we do not wish to be reminded of. We learn to drown it out and set our mind's clock to school bells, dinners and Coronation Street.

It was as if I just didn't acclimatise until Jamie was born. I had no friends to speak of. Of course, there had been the usual pairing off

41

with my mother's friends' children, but that had always gone spectacularly wrong. Like the time I removed all the Sindy doll heads and put them in the cistern at the local bank manager's house. That, and other attempts to find me a friend, ended with my mother gritting her teeth. When we got home, after an attempt at asking what was wrong with me, she would mutter to my father about it in hushed tones in my presence. There was talk about me going back to Dublin to see the woman in the room. Older local kids called me names when they passed, as I played alone outside the house or lay in the field next door with Polly, watching the clouds. They'd throw things in at me and laugh.

'Spastic,' they'd shout.

If anyone in the family noticed they never said.

I honestly never cared, and I knew then and know now, despite O'Hara's attempts to explain it, that they threw things at me because they felt more rejected by me than I did by them.

It was all irrelevant anyway, after Jamie arrived.

Jamie and I would lie for hours making popping noises with our mouths, and he loved the sound of the piano playing; his favourite tune was *Good King Wenceslas*, which made him laugh.

As he grew up, I'd crawl with him and the dog. I'd repeat his silly first words. We were together at last. The only happy childhood memories that I can hold onto were formed after he was born.

Everyone noticed the change in me. Especially Mona, who conveniently forgot that I had been withdrawn all the time she had known me, not just in the month after Jerome and Deborah died. Her smiled broadened when she saw us playing.

'The little brother you never had,' she'd say, but never in front of my sisters.

I don't know where Jamie had been between this life and the next: perhaps floating in limbo, perhaps somewhere else where I wasn't and he couldn't tell me, or rather, I had forgotten too much to be able to understand if he did.

If I had been able perhaps I would have the answers now to all the questions I am left with. Not that O'Hara would accept them of course.

Back then, Jamie and I understood each other. In that time, in that present, we were happy, and that's all that matters now. The present is everything; the adult preoccupation with the thoughts of their children's future can spoil even the most innocent fun.

We ended up sleeping in the same bed half the time, and he would talk gibberish to me and I'd respond in what became our secret language. When it rained we'd hide under the covers, pretending we were back in the depths of the sea where we had been happy before. Mona would come into the room and remind us dinner was ready, or that it was time for my piano practice. Apart from that we were left to our own devices.

8

Before Jamie started real school we got to go on a proper summer sun holiday to Torremolinos. We had a two-bedroom apartment overlooking a beach that stretched for miles. I thought we had moved there and was excited to be back at the seafront. My sisters laughed amongst themselves as they slathered themselves with bronzer. They lay on their towels like fly traps and stared at the boys passing by. The waves lapped against the pristine yellow sand that every night was turned over with diggers.

Mona and George tried to cover up the first strains in their relationship with lurid cocktails by the pool on the first day. George went to the pub by himself on the second day and stayed there until dinnertime. Mona stayed on the sun loungers reading. Jamie and I didn't play with the other kids; they stayed away, just like the kids at home. Even in another country there was a magic circle around us that no one could penetrate.

On the second last day, we found a body washed up on the beach, brown and bloated. The man looked peaceful. We stared at him for a while, and then began to include him in our games and our conversation. We placed shells on his eyes and whispered in his ears in our private language. It was as if he belonged with us.

It took Mona awhile to notice what was happening.

'Jesus, Jesus, Jesus, George, George!' she screamed over and over until he came.

She then dragged Jamie away; George grabbed me.

The only thing that traumatised us that day was her hysteria. She had to be subdued with pills by the hotel doctor.

Later that day I saw the police remove the body from the hotel window. When we returned to Ireland she would purse her lips and leave the room when we played it out over and over again.

O'Hara says that the seahorse fixation is directly related to this incident. He says this incident, coupled so closely with my parents' death, left me comparing their mangled made-up faces with this man who had looked so peaceful. He says I assumed people would be peaceful and happy if they died under the sea, compared to those who died in a brutal car crash. Again, I agreed with him eventually, though I laugh now when I think of it. I feel sorry for him. He has no recollection of his ancestral past or understanding of who he really is, or what it is to be and feel and know the patterns of this life, and the one before, and the one after. He explains away everything with his learned rationality.

The only psychological damage that occurred in Spain was caused by my sisters bitching and Mona and George C's awkwardness. Spain could have been Mars to George, although the food in the hotel was chicken and chips and burgers. Mona was obviously embarrassed by his loud questioning of all that was not Irish and his obvious distrust of the place.

O'Hara says I had a fear of separation from Jamie, as George was my relative, not Mona. Although I would never have even spoken to him had it not been for the marriage. Jamie didn't seem to notice, and it never crossed his mind that I might leave him stranded on this rock.

Life went on at home, though Mona stopped going to the pub with George. She immersed herself in schoolwork and George had the farm. He went to the pub earlier and earlier. They rowed about the house; George wanted to move into the dormer. There was only the four of us now he said. Mona rolled her eyes and pursed her lips. Then he'd leave for the pub when she got the better of his argument.

Jamie and I played on together, oblivious in our underwater fantasy life. By the time he went to school, being the now-Principal's children set us apart even more in the small village. Teachers' children were pariahs, informants and snobs. Their parents of course wanted them to play with the Principal's children, and dutifully made them invite us to every birthday party. We sat in the corner, occasionally making forays to the party table for limp jam sandwiches and weak Miwadi. We sat waiting for the sea to rise up and take us back to peace.

9

Mona and George moved into separate rooms but played on with the let's-keep-our-marriage-together-for-the-sake-of-the-Catholic-Church. The church was, after all, her employer. Mona had her job, George had his booze, and he wasn't violent.

'He snores,' she said unconvincingly, as if I had asked her about it.

'You'll understand when you're older.'

I was with Jamie the first time it happened. I knew there was something wrong instantly, even before I could see it. I felt him leave, though when I turned to him on the couch he was still sitting there. My mouth gaped in reaction to his sudden absence. There was a vacant expression on his face; he rocked back and forth, his eyes rolling in his head.

'Jamie, Jamie,' I called. 'Don't leave me here.'

He came out of it after a few minutes.

'Where were you?' I said. 'Where were you?'

He looked at me blankly and turned back to the television.

Mona saw it the second time. We were watching TV again. He was rocking, then he snapped back suddenly and fell sideways off the chair. It was worse than before, his body spasmed and twisted upward, his face hit the side of the chair leg. She stood back, not knowing what to do; this was not a school situation where she could take charge. This was her son. Then she looked at me.

'Marina, Marina, look at me, has this happened before? Tell me, answer me.'

I saw her hand rise towards my face as if in slow motion; the slap made both of us reel. She turned away and went to the phone to call the ambulance.

After endless tests and hospital appointments, Jamie was diagnosed with epilepsy and put on medication.

It is Monday again; I know that because there is a bigger gap between O'Hara's visits. There is beige chicken and orange carrots, carrots Julienne. I laugh and think of Sandra and Jules. O'Hara asks me about them when he comes. I don't answer. He waits, and then rebounds with one word.

'Puberty,' he says, as if off a checklist. 'How was puberty for you, Marina?' he asks. This is an easier subject. I know what I should say.

'Hmmm, difficult,' I say.

He is pleased. 'Yes, for many patients here it is a difficult time, the onset of many symptoms, your childhood leaves abruptly.'

I nod. He continues.

'Tell me about your relationship with Jamie.'

I look at him sideways, 'Can we go somewhere else?' I say.

He is pleased. He has been trying to get me to work in his office for weeks, longer, since I came.

I need to show him I am improving. I know he will see this as a good sign and he does.

'Tomorrow,' he says. 'Meet me in my office tomorrow and we'll go from there.' His tone is distinctly brighter, brisker. He stands up and says, '10am, I shall send a nurse to fetch you,' he pauses, 'Well done Marina.'

He leaves.

I have given him nothing today, but have gauged his response correctly. I am learning. I turn over and try to get back to sleep, back into the dream I was having, I try to stay submerged. I think about puberty.

O'Hara has told me before that I should write in his absence. They have given me blunt pencils but no sharpener, and headed A4 sheets ruled in blue. A picture of the 'house' on the top of every page. It makes it look more like a country hotel than the expensive nut house it is. I sit up and write, then decide against it, scribbling out the first word: Hippocampus. He may come when I sleep and read it.

My mouth tastes of burnt toast and the chemical aftertaste of pills. I am groggy; I will talk to O'Hara about this. I drift back to sleep.

I am back in the shower in Mona's; Jamie is at the door. I hear Mona scolding him, telling him I need my privacy. I look down and see what separates us; I scrub until it hurts, scrubbing them away.

The boys at school began to tease me after that, grabbing me at lunchtime. I was truly alone from the first day of secondary school, our second most official separation. I left every morning early on the bus. I sat up the front, seeking the protection of the driver. Trying to be oblivious to the shouting down the back, practising piano in my head. I dreaded lunchtime and tried to find an empty classroom to read my book, or an empty cubicle where I could sit undetected. Unless it was raining, when everyone congregated inside, except the very brave. I'd sit in the cubicle on the toilet, my legs going numb, imagining my body as flexible as a conger eel, diving down through the u bend, wiggling free and swimming through the pipes, arms out in front through the green, kicking my legs until I emerged in the sea, swimming underwater, kicking off my shoes and undoing my tie and swimming, swimming away from this place and all of them.

I always told him we could go back, or that the sea would come back for us. I told him before he could speak, before he could tell me first. I told him about it, but he knew of course. I was just saying it out loud to comfort us both. Underneath the covers where he'd be still and not cry. Mona would leave us there. I was no longer alone in my high chair, staring at the sea, waiting for him to come like the sword from the lake.

After the medication took him away again, I read a book Mona had explaining epilepsy. I found the diagram of the centre of the brain, where the epilepsy lay. It was Hippocampus, the seahorse, the centre of the brain. The one who had caused all the trouble by climbing up onto the shore first. I knew Hippocampus was angry because we wanted to go back, and Hippocampus was going to kill Jamie to stop us. We would go back together or it would come for us. The sea was coming back for us I said. Then Hippocampus took him, shaking and rocking. And then the doctors gave him the drugs, and then he was lost. He didn't remember anymore.

So I left him before he was destroyed. I retreated further and further back, retracting, alone, until the day I walked past him, unheeding, as I got off the bus where he was always waiting, as the local children stood staring as he shook on the ground; I walked past alone and walked further away because Hippocampus was angry, and we stood and we lay and we shook. We became I. It was I and only I who walked away. He lay in the ditch jerking sideways; they stood around him staring. His red hair against the green, his mouth bleeding. They jeered at me as I walked away.

'There goes the other spastic,' they shouted.

So I continued on my path. I decided to go forward, alone, like Hippocampus wanted, step by step, walking through frozen water, my limbs trying to disobey me. The breath in my lungs solidifying, rising to my throat; I swallowed it down to my hardened heart, I blinked back the tears, squeezing my eyes to stop them bringing me back to him. Biting the lip that threatened to call out in our secret language, to try to bring him back again. I went into the house and said nothing. I went straight to my room. One of the kids came and told Mona eventually. She never asked me had I seen him that day. He never asked me either, but he knew.

The seas are rising but too slowly, too slowly. When it comes I will pretend I hadn't known. But I know it will come. Because water must win in the end, water is the centre of all, even Hippocampus. The seas will cover the world again and we will all be underwater again, where we started. The experiment has failed. Though water knows we can start again; we have before. This time Hippocampus will call the *appendages to join it and walk forward in a different direction, a more peaceful one than this, and then water can rest again.*

I avoided them all until it was time to leave. Mona put it down to teenage hormones and ignored it all.

The nurse comes to take me to O'Hara's office. I dig my nails into my hands and follow her. I concentrate on the heels of her white shoes as I follow her down the corridor.

Part 2

Sharp Waves

10

I went to London looking for something new, the answer to life in what was the opposite of the village. I could not bear the blankness that was Jamie. I could not live with my betrayal. When I had flown over for the audition I had smelled the freedom. I had sensed an escape. This was a place where betrayal was commonplace, a place where I belonged. A scholarship to the Royal College of Music in London was a prestigious thing that Mona and I had worked for my whole life, according to her. Even my violin lessons of late had been geared towards the second instrument requirement. It made the local paper amid the adverts that dominated it, but should have been alongside the death notices. Now I was of age I had inherited quite a sum of money from my late parents, so the cost of living in London on a scholarship wasn't an issue.

Mona and Jamie came with me and we cried a lot, even Jamie cried through his medicated haze. We went to the supermarket before they left. Mona put away the shopping from the many carrier bags. Then she folded up the bags and put them in the space between the washing machine and the worktop. I never used them again. I hugged Mona and Jamie stiffly goodbye.

They left me there in the student campus that I was to share with another student. The pain of old resurfaced like a tsunami. How could I explain how much I missed a drugged-up eleven year old with a lurching feeling that made me want to vomit and that followed me like a grey cloud. I had to crawl forward by myself so that Hippocampus would leave Jamie alone.

'I'm Mill,' the girl said. 'I'm from Derbyshire.'

'Oh right,' I said, as if I knew where it was. 'I'm Marina, what's your instrument?' I asked, though I could see the cello case through her open bedroom door.

Her main instrument was the cello, but her second was the

piano. It was good that we had something in common. She was to be my first female friend, albeit for a very brief time. We became instant friends as first years do, adrift in an alien landscape.

I adored the freedom of London, and it blew through the hole in my chest and distracted it somewhat. I would jump nihilistically onto the edge of the wall of the bridge crossing the Thames. Mill would scream and I'd sing out loud because I could, and because I knew I wouldn't see the passers-by again at mass or at the shop. They wouldn't know Mona or comment on how odd or highly strung I was, a musical genius, a bereaved daughter losing her mind in a small hamlet in rural Ireland. People didn't even blink when I walked through London singing old Rolling Stones songs. George had played them religiously on a Sunday afternoon after the pub.

Mill and I lived life in a typical student fashion, tumbling day after day after day between dirty laundry on the floor, borrowed mascara, bad food from the canteen, lectures, and, of course, music. We met all kinds of musical prodigies of every persuasion, and it was at an impromptu concert that I first met Jules.

He sat alone and looked as pained as I felt. He wore a long earring, a wooden seahorse that told me to follow. He wore a series of T-shirts that featured a monkey wrench on them or simply said 'The Monkey Wrench Gang'. I assumed it was a band I'd never heard of. Despite all the other distractions of my new life, it was him I thought of when I lay at night awake in bed. The unfamiliar orange light from the street slanted through the Venetian blinds. The glance we had exchanged had burned into my retinas like the image of the sun on a bright day, when you look at it by accident and blink purple and yellow perfect suns. It illuminated the darkness of the centre of my mind and blasted out all else.

11

Jules evaded me purposefully after our eyes met that night, but this did not discourage me. Mill fanned my obsession and breathlessly led me to places she knew he would be. I found out that the violin was his first instrument, so we did not cross paths as often as we could have. He was in second year so we didn't share any lectures. This just served to cultivate my obsession further. He did not live on campus as I did, arriving instead by tube from a mysterious address to which no one seemed to be privy. Mill said she had asked around, and it was said that he either lived with his mother, or in a squat in Holland Park with a bunch of eco warriors.

My obsession with Jules and my music filled my entire being. I began to fixate on Jules' beauty in public, and composed a soundtrack to him on paper.

I tell this once to O'Hara; he asks me to sing the soundtrack, to hum it. I do.

'It sounds like classical music composed by Morrissey,' he says, in a rare moment of humour.

Mill nudged me more than once to warn me that I was staring at Jules. I even persuaded her to help me follow him home. We got his timetable from another second year. One Friday we waited for him on the entrance steps, giggling and trying to act casual. He passed us at five past four, alone as usual. It was starting to turn towards London twilight already. We followed him from a distance, occasionally ducking behind the street awnings covering fruit and vegetables, but only for effect. We banged into an old West Indian woman who sucked her teeth at us as; we laughed hysterically, apologising. Then we saw him turn into the Gloucester Road tube station. We lost him on an escalator that towered so high that I was unable to run up it for sheer dizziness.

He told me later that he knew we had been following him, that our giggles had given it away. He said he had lost us by stepping into a kiosk and then coming back down to the same platform, until it was clear we were returning to the college. He said that I was obviously trying to draw attention to myself, which was typical of the deceit that he began to see in everything I did.

We finally got to talk in the Students' Union bar, where I giddily plunked myself between him and the edge of the crowd. Drunkenly, I asked him outright what his name was. He answered me in a disinterested fashion. He even added a fake surname too, Jules Carr I think he said. We talked about the environment mostly; he too mentioned the seas rising up, but he said that he was going to stop them. He said that there was a war on, us versus the sea, us versus Capitalism. I seemed to be part of an 'us' again. I was two months into my obsession and determined not to return after Christmas if he did not kiss me, the agony was so unbearable. My innocence at this point was profound; I had never even been kissed before. I could not deny my need for his attention, however slight. I felt I was swimming in sludge, and being with him made it clear and safe. From then on, I felt important; he had finally spoken to me. I believed then that his solitude had been imposed by the group and not him. I was determined to join him in this splendid isolation.

The night came to an end with a kiss. Our heads leaned towards one another out on the pavement, under the street lamp where we dallied after the Students' Union bar was closed. Mill led a round of drunken applause. In response, Jules turned heel and walked off, with no goodbye or explanation. I was left drunken, dejected, and hating Mill with violence for sending him away.

12

I saw Jules again a week later in the canteen where I was picking at an inedible pasta bake. I didn't go to him, he came to me, and wordlessly kissed me. Tears dripped down my face and mingled at our lips, his dry and rough. I felt like screaming and running out onto the foggy London streets. Taking him with me by the hand until we were finally lost in the maze of streets running across the A to Z. Until we ran off the map. I played the soundtrack in my mind, and I laid down the final track later that night. I still consider it one of my finest pieces, although I don't play anymore.

He stopped kissing me and leaned back, looking at me, his dark eyes laughing from behind his dreadlocks and pale face. I couldn't stop shaking; he took my hand, led me outside, and for the first time we really talked. He told me he liked me, and had liked me since even before I could trace seeing him for the first time. He said that he was afraid of relationships, that they were strange things that grew like black mould across the blank music sheets in his mind and interfered with his creative purpose. They also interfered with the war for the environment, the defence of the earth, which he had suffered greatly for. Despite that, however, he couldn't forget me. I was honoured that he was giving all this up for me. Turning his back on this self-imposed mandate, all for the hope of me. Just as I had turned my back on Jamie.

We skipped our lectures and sat in the college grounds under the magnolia tree, and we kissed so hard I thought my lips would bleed. I was falling and did not feel the damp of the grass soaking my jeans, only him. Our mingled breathing drowned out the ever-present drone of aeroplanes.

Then he abruptly broke away and declared that he must go. I calmly arranged to meet him the next day, still in a trance, still overwhelmed by his presence. I returned, dazed, to the flat and Mill.

'I saw you come out of canteen together!' she squealed.

I smiled back.

'Tell me all!'

There was nothing to tell.

'How do you feel?'

'Tired,' I said.

What I felt was pain, but pain like a spot that's coming up on the skin, that you keep touching and wincing, because the touch jars something beyond physicality and this world. I went to bed and stared at the ceiling, unable to sleep. I repeated every minute of our embrace and our conversation like a slideshow in my mind. Even after replaying them on repeat, I realised I still knew nothing about him. All I had was that which I, or rather Mill, had garnered around the college. That and our embraces.

Next day's lectures went over my head. I rang home and spoke to Mona. She put Jamie on, who didn't say anything. She took the phone back and told me that he missed me badly, but the drugs had had to be increased since I left. I thought she would have been able to detect the seismic change in me since last night, but she didn't. I found when I put down the receiver that the lurch of homesickness was more removed than usual.

I went to meet Jules in a bar called The Churchill Arms in Holland Park. I arrived nervously early, and sat eating peanuts until it seemed like he wouldn't turn up. I only breathed out when he did. He seemed different here, away from the college. He was more innocent and boy-like. We held hands and I drank the Happy Hour cocktails on offer, steering clear of innuendos like *Sex on the Beach* and *Long Good Screw*. He drank Guinness. We laughed at the college and the lecturers, but he evaded my questions about his personal life. Then people he knew came in, more dreadlocks, more monkey wrenches on T-shirts and on leaflets.

He introduced the one who sat beside us.

'Marina, Mark.'

'Alright Marina, you Irish then?'

'Yes,' I replied.

'Nuclear-free living,' he said wistfully, then turned away to talk to the rest of them.

'I met him at Tilbury,' Jules said.

I didn't know what he meant, but smiled and nodded anyway.

Afterwards, I asked Jules back to my flat, and he drunkenly agreed. Mill made faces of surprised shock behind his back when she came home, but went straight to her room. I made him chicory coffee and we sat on the tiny sofa. A sofa more suited to a school for young offenders than student residences. We furtively groped and kissed, crushing our bodies uncomfortably against the wooden arms.

I squeezed my eyes shut and leaned back. His breath was all I could hear, panting; weirdly, it reminded me of Polly. My back crushed against the wooden arms of the sofa. His hands were huge, hot on my skin, his breath then on my neck, on my ribs. I arched up as if to glue myself to him, to swim into him. I twisted sideways.

'Fuck,' he said, jumping up and shaking his hand. 'You caught my hand on the sofa.'

The spell was broken.

'I'm sorry,' I whispered, not wanting Mill to hear about my failure. She had told me all about what to do; she had had sex before, and had even had a boyfriend.

'We can go to my room,' I pleaded, getting up and taking his hand.

He flinched back; his face had blackened. 'No, I better go home.' He tucked his shirt in and kissed me chastely on the mouth. 'See you tomorrow,' he said, as if nothing had happened.

I slumped down again onto the couch; my heart thumped. I didn't answer Mill when she called out from her room.

He started calling around to the flat every evening. Mill got bored of the exile to her room and the lack of Jules' response to her questions about the Earth First! movement. She tried to engage with tales about the protest against the motorway near her home in Twyford Downs a few years before.

'Were you there yourself?' she asked.

He pretended not to hear her.

So she took the hint, and disappeared to the bar or to other students' flats.

I improved on the violin, but I was never as good as Jules. In alternating sequences Mozart went back to back with Nirvana. We talked about climate change, protests and Kurt Cobain, but not about Jules. It was as if he wanted to be there only in the present-here-and-now of the flat. That cold, hostile, polyvinyl environment that stayed barren despite the Portobello market rag rugs, throws and posters that Mill and I had bought on our first Sunday in London. It still retained that classroom feel, with plastic grey venetian blinds and grey-speckled work surfaces.

He began to stay over too, as we often only realised the last tube had gone hours after it had. We didn't have sex at first, though he was the one who was reluctant, not me. We'd reach a point, then he'd stop and tell me he didn't know what I wanted from him. His words cut deep and twisted. I'd try to think of a way to make him feel better. This was one of his favourite subjects, his inadequate self. He talked into the night about how his music wasn't good enough, and how he had only got into college because of the school he went to. It had been a comprehensive he said, and his music teacher had helped him get in. There was nothing about family or home; no matter how much I hinted, or even outright asked, he wouldn't tell; that all came later. So I imagined it instead.

I imagined a wonderful, aristocratic family, Jules their only son, fallen on hard times due to crashing stocks and shares. Or some other tragedy, perhaps fraud committed by the family butler. Their lives played out to a classical soundtrack, where a weeping, pale, beautiful mother pulled down all the blinds and took to her four-poster bed. The music slowed as she wept for the better days while his father drank brandy in the study and watched his son out the window, heading for this comprehensive school that he knew would end their way of life forever. Deeper, slower, ominous notes crept into my imagined soundtrack as they were forced to take in lodgers, but the music lightened as one of the lodgers taught Jules the violin. Jules, or Julian the Second as he would have been titled, or the fourth or fifth. This kindly lodger, a PhD student perhaps called Phillip, coached young Jules, who practised each night in the half-light. Scrounging his meals by visiting the various lodgers, as all the rent money went on brandy. Eventually, my imaginary Jules learned to collect the rent directly from them to buy groceries. He tried to entice his mother from her room with cooked meals and violin solos. She'd slump in flat notes down the dusty stairs and into the back kitchen where she would sit herself down, clearly drugged, and eat only sweet things. Perhaps nibbling on grapes and reminiscing about holidays to Italy. The evenings ending in a violin solo and tears as she imagined herself at the ball.

I imagined all this as I lay awake, watching him under the streetlight that shone through the Venetian blind. I would have loved to explore all this further with Mill, but she had practically disappeared from the flat. Jules usually got up early, and was gone before I awoke late and shuffled out of my dream-filled nights. I was reluctant to leave these dreams, where scenarios more exotic than ever played out the details of his life. I believed that I knew innately why he had become so closed. I had invented and dreamed myriads of lives for him, past and present and future, so it no longer mattered what he withheld from me.

While I dreamed he slept, and I soothed myself thinking about him and his aristocratic life. I didn't make any other friends and he had none at the college. So when Christmas came I had to tear myself away and go home. Jules left me to the airport on the tube, and was as vague as ever about where and when we'd meet after Christmas. He murmured about the evils of aeroplane travel and asked why I hadn't taken the boat.

14

I spent the whole time dreaming about Jules while I was at home. I played his voice over and over in my head, shut in my room. Jamie was thin and lost and drugged-up. We lay in my room listening to tapes of Jules playing the violin, either that or Nirvana. I told Jamie about Seattle and the Earth Liberation Front. Jamie had got taller and thinner and, despite his frequent fits, made me feel calm for moments at a time.

Jules only rang a few times. I'd sit on the stairs, freezing and listening to him rant about how awful London was at Christmas. How corporatism had taken over. Jamie would stand and stare at the top of the stairs, looking frightened by my silence. Mona would come by and roll her eyes and shoo him away while George C made jokes.

Mona tried in vain a few times to engage me in conversation about these mysterious phone calls. 'So, who was that on the phone?' she asked casually, while making toast for Jamie. 'Anyone special I should know about?'

'Just someone from college,' I said, reaching past her into the bread bin.

'A boyfriend?' she asked, smiling.

I shrugged and took the bread as it was and turned back into the sitting room.

What could I tell her? She was pleased he was at the college too, though; I could tell. As if this were an advert for a perfect match, and I laughed at how she would react to Jules' hair.

I was shocked at hers. Mona had got older, and I noticed it more as we spoke; grey was appearing, and without me she had begun to dress like every other woman in the town.

My sisters arrived back on Christmas Eve, just before mass. Christmas Mass was like the auditions for The Stepford Wives. I sat with Jamie, feeling the hymns hurtle through me and over the balcony, to the high dome above all our heads. Sleep was all I wanted in the drowsy, packed warmness in the crowd, the air full of incense. It reminded me of the funeral.

15

It was from this distance that I began to learn some more about Jules. I had to trail to another country to do so. He mentioned his mum but no dad, and revealed that he lived on an estate. I pictured this alternative scenario too, and was delighted to indulge in it over the course of the holidays.

Jules now became part of a single-parent family, living in a waste-strewn council estate. Endless, soulless, grey block after block of flats, only delineated by the clothes-lines strewn across the balconies. He was sensitive from day one again, clearly musically talented to the trained ear but ignored by his chain-smoking mother. Who fed him spam and chips. Leaving him in the flat for hours alone while she paraded around the local pubs, looking for boyfriends. Or a new dad, as she'd tell him on her drunken return. When she brought these potentials home she only ignored him even more. Rejected by his malnourished peers, he found solace in music and in the natural world. He longed for the wilderness. He wandered for miles in search of rivers and mountains, having to make do with empty factories and brownfield sites.

At school, he was heralded a genius and helped by friendly teachers. One of his mother's lovers had introduced him to the violin. While his mother continued to remain oblivious to all this, he shone brightly from the grey concrete. A mother and an estate filled me up like marshmallows to the throat. I felt I knew him intimately, and between his rants I pressed him to say he missed me when no one was listening; he grunted and said he did. Jamie would turn and pad silently back to my room when this happened. I always felt him leave.

I missed Jules, though I could not see a future ahead for us. This agonised me. I pictured myself in a white bedroom in the future, with a white bedspread, floral curtains and a net at the window, lying despairingly on the bed alone, trapped and unhappy. I was not with

Jules anymore, but still loved him. I thought I would love him forever.

We had finally had sex before I left. It was awkward and I felt I had not been experienced enough, and he had obviously done it before, awkwardly taking what seemed like hours to finish. Perhaps I wasn't sexy enough, and so resolved on reading about it over Christmas. I had found a book in Fionnuala's room: *'Red Hot Lover: give your man what he needs to make him stay not stray'*. I stuffed it in the cupboard above my wardrobe among my college books so Mona wouldn't find it and frighten the life out of George C. Though I didn't suppose they had sex anymore, as they had had no kids since. According to my book they probably did, and that's what kept them together. I was sure that was true, so I learned the secret of what knickers I should wear among other things, not my sensible cotton ones that Mona had bought me. I felt awkward hiding this around Jamie and I began to lock the door; it bewildered him. I heard Mona mutter to him in the hall about ladies' private things. I heard him shuffle downstairs and into the back garden, into the cold and the rain with the dog. Polly was grey and lame now but she was Jamie's sole companion, as she had been mine.

George brought us to the beach. It seemed smaller than before. The car park bin was overflowing with rubbish. But for a moment I forgot my confusion and aching, and felt I was home again. I walked to the edge of the water. I stood and stared at the grey sea, churning and breaking on the rocks, as George threw sticks, which the dog ignored but seemed to be aware of. She whined as each one flew into the air. I stuck my foot into the water with my boots still on and Jamie followed suit. George looked alarmed, as if his drugged-up son would have a seizure and fall into the waves, so he gruffly told us that it was time to go. I climbed over the rocks back to the car instead of taking the path. The rock pools looked like puddles now. Jamie followed the path with the dog. My flight was the next day.

16

I arrived back and half-hoped to be met at the airport, but couldn't see his face in the crowds. He told me later that he had been there, watching in case I had gone to Ireland with somebody else. The crowds made me nauseous after the nothingness of country life. I had not been persuaded to go to the Christmas sales in the city. I got the tube back to central London and made my way across to the college by red bus. Jules arrived an hour later into the frozen bleak flat and we fell into each other's arms. I declared I would never go home again and he held me tighter. We got undressed and into bed and lay under the cold sheets, under the strange glow of the streetlights.

He told me months later that he had come to meet me at the airport to surprise me. But when he saw me emerge he had stepped back and watched me, as I took everything in and readjusted to it all. It was fascinating to watch me without me knowing. He said his Dad had used to take him bird watching in the South Downs when he was alive. Once, some ravens killed a bird just out of the nest. His dad had made him watch.

'Survival of the fittest, son,' he had said. That was the last thing he had said to him before he died too.

He said that sometimes I was like the little brown bird, fallen from the nest, going about my business, oblivious to all the ravens that surrounded me.

I ventured a question about his mother and he answered painfully. He told me that he lived with his mother and had been trapped there over Christmas with her, watching ghastly Christmas television. I asked him more about her. He said that she worked in the civil service, doing something or other in an office. He told me that they lived in Croydon. I jokingly asked when I would get to meet her. He surprised me when he said soon. I was happy.

We slept in each other's arms all night, and I woke to find him there in the morning. I could hear him in the kitchen. I went out to see him cleaning the sink. I suggested we go out for breakfast. We headed for the local greasy London cafe. Jules ordered two veggie fry-ups. There were pools of grease sliding off the fried eggs, tinned plum tomatoes and soft margarine on thin slices of bread. All served on dirty white plates plunked on the pale, blue-speckled white Formica table.

When we were finished, he said we were going to meet his mother. We got the train from Victoria. An empty midday stopping train, running along by the soulless grey blocks where I'd pictured him once. I was relieved he didn't live there, and thought that at least I would not have to introduce to Mona an English council estate boy who was after my inheritance. Even still, I never told him about the money. I found it embarrassing and wrong and barely touched it, living only on the interest and my scholarship.

We got off the train and walked down soulless streets and into an estate of Barratt homes; they were all the same. This was stranger to me even than central London. He pulled out his key from under a pot of geraniums by the door, still bright in the January frost. His mother called out, an abrasive, nasally voice that pierced through my dreamy state.

'Julian, is that you?'

She came forward into the darkened hallway, drying a glass and squinting into the half-light at me. Jules introduced us awkwardly and brushed by us upstairs. She invited me into the sitting room. I searched around for pictures immediately, and grinned at his face in eighties haircuts and clothing, looking down at me angelically. The music trophies clustered in a huge leaded-glass cabinet.

I sat down on the cream leather couch, camouflaged by the cream walls and carpet. I imagined that this was where Jules had found his love of all things black. His mother introduced herself as

Sandra. She was blonde and about fifty. She asked me the usual questions about Ireland.

'London must seem ever so big,' she remarked.

She probably saw me through the eyes of bad soap operas, an Ireland that had no tumble dryers and that had donkeys on every street.

However, I was just grateful to be there, high on nervous energy and distracted, half-wondering where Jules had disappeared to.

'So what do your parents think of you being here then?' she asked.

'Oh, they're both dead now,' I said.

'Julian's father is dead too, but of course you know that.'

I let her talk, feigning knowledge by nodding.

'Pancreatic cancer it was. He went fast. Poor Julian was only ten.'

Out of the corner of my eye I saw The Daily Mail. I waited for the onslaught of comments about The IRA and the like but they didn't come; well, not that night anyway.

'There's two Irish women where I work. Downstairs in the canteen there's a woman called Mary and there's Irish Nicola on the 6th floor. With the purple suit and the hair?'

She seemed disappointed that I didn't know them and changed the subject. 'I told Wendy at the office Julian was bringing home an Irish girl. Well at least she won't have them dreadlocks like the other ones I said. Don't suit him at all.' 'So are you staying the night?' she asked. 'I've only a single bed in the spare room. But not because I'm fuddy duddy mind!'

'I got used to having him around at Christmas.'

My answer was interrupted by the return of Jules. She switched the rhetorical question to him. He shrugged his shoulders at the news of our impending sojourn.

'That's settled then,' she said brightly.

'Marina, do you want to come to Marks and Spencer's to grab a bottle of wine?'

I got up awkwardly and stood by the door while she got ready. She fluffed her hair up in the hall mirror before she got to the door. I side-shuffled to let her open it, then shuffled around her. When we got into the car she checked her hair again.

'It's a different blonde to my usual,' she said before she started the engine.

She was a terrible driver; we were beeped at twice in the two minutes it took to get to the shopping centre. She didn't seem to notice.

We entered the brightly-lit food hall together and went straight to the ready meals section. A vegetarian bake for Jules and me. I picked up a bottle of red wine and tried to pay for it. She shunned my attempted contribution and took it from me. As she paid, she exchanged pleasantries with the checkout girl; she seemed to know her. She admitted she came here a lot, saying cooking for one was no fun and wasn't Marks a godsend. She supposed we didn't have that sort of thing in Ireland, and was disappointed to hear that we did. As if that took away from the flavour of Marks' ready meals.

We drowsed in front of the television as she microwaved, and Jules filled in the gaps between the pings with a heavy silence. He disapproved of the ready meals but he ate them anyway.

17

I thought then that Jules was now revealed to me. He had lost his mystery. I knew what no one else in the college did.

I tried to tell Mill.

'He's a fucking psycho, Marina,' she said, rolling her eyes.

I went to my room.

'I'm moving out,' she called through the door. 'You'll learn soon enough. Ask him what he said to me in the canteen.'

I didn't come out.

I didn't find out where she went and no one else moved in, as it was halfway through the year. I didn't have to pay extra, though I could have afforded it anyway. I could have afforded a quayside apartment but I liked the security and ordinariness of the college, and it kept my finances secret from everyone, especially Jules' friends.

I had gone to the squat in Holland Park with him; I was surprised by how ordinary it was. From the outside, it just looked like a huge Edwardian House. I had expected a boarded-up wreck covered in graffiti. Inside it was sparsely furnished, the walls painted with bright murals.

Jules' friends dreamed of the simple life: living in self-made tents, benders, with wood fires. They built simple structures with willow branches and tarpaulin in the huge, overgrown garden. They practised the survival skills they said would be necessary when global warming drove humans out of the cities. They warned that the melting ice in the poles would turn into a flood and drown all the corporate scum who would not survive as they could.

Jules had shrugged when I told him Mill had moved out. He said he had never trusted her anyway, and wasn't surprised. I was closed off from the world of a girlfriend just as it had begun. It made me sad; she didn't even speak when we passed each other on the stairs. I began to think that Jules had been right when he said she had never really been my friend. I avoided her as much as possible, and tried not to meet her eyes when I did see her.

So then it was just Jules and me, interspersed with lectures and time in the music practice rooms. It had always been like this, Jamie and me, now it was me and Jules, so it suited me. It was just like home. But I still missed Jamie. I told Jules about when we were little and in bed, and I tried to tell him about before but I wasn't sure anymore: was it just a game we had invented, I had invented? Jules told me about Sea Shepherd, an eco warrior man on a boat, defending the lives of all the creatures of the sea however he had to do it.

I rang Jamie sometimes, in the mornings before school. We didn't say much, then Mona would take back the phone and tell me who had died or got married. Their faces filled my mind in an abstract way; I was never sure if I was thinking of the right person. I found out that Fionnuala was getting married that summer in the village church. I decided I would bring Jules home then and said as much. Mona was pleased to hear I still had a boyfriend, but said she hoped it wouldn't keep me from my studies.

18

Jules begged me not to go home that Easter so I stayed, despite the fact that Fionnuala had arranged for me to been fitted for a bridesmaid's dress. Mona was awkward on the phone; she was upset but wouldn't say so.

Jules and I did nothing much, listened to music, made music, made love, ate and slept. We went to Sandra's on Easter Sunday for a roast dinner in lieu of mass. Jules barely spoke to either of us. He ate dinner with us then left for his room. It made me feel guilty and uneasy. I decided that he must blame Sandra for his father's death, plunging the shallow depths of my understanding of psychology.

So we watched bad TV, and I got a rundown of the world according to the Daily Mail. Sandra shook her dyed-blonde permed hair and pursed her lips as she spoke with surety on how terrorists were running the streets and gypsies were pick-pocketing everyone. I forced a smile on my lips and resisted the need to argue. That Sunday she was as near as I could get to Jules.

He'd whisper in my ear at night, clutching me tight, saying I was his only love. How I was everything to him and he'd die without me, he wouldn't be able to live or make music. I was flattered, and I felt the same way about him. Our love was painful and intense and filled up my thoughts all day at college, and in the lonely Sundays on Sandra's couch.

After Easter lectures began to blur, so I started skipping the more difficult ones. I ate Fruit Pastilles for breakfast. I ate them one colour at a time, trying not to chew them, but to suck the sugar from the sharp edges and find their softness. I watched daytime television, American talk shows that featured country folk fighting and having endless affairs. I wondered about sex. Jules had become increasingly frantic and scratched my back with his nails, and more than once he had called me a bitch. The first time he said it I had stopped mid-thrust, shocked, and wiggled out from under him. He had got up and left, so next time I said nothing. I thought about Jamie lying on the ground, and the blackness, and I knew I deserved it. I knew that Jules saw through me. My parents were dead and I didn't care, Jamie was lost and I had walked away. At least now I felt something.

The accusations came after that: he said that I would leave him, he said that I was seeing someone else. Summer was coming fast. I had asked him to come with me to my sister's wedding before Easter. He had agreed, but had said that my sisters would hate him. That they wouldn't understand him. He also reminded me that he didn't know anyone else there. When he finally agreed to go, he made me promise to stay with him all the time. Then he persuaded me to come back after the wedding and spend the summer in London.

I applied for a job on the campus, as a receptionist for the holidaymakers who stayed in the residences in the summer months. Also, it meant that I didn't have to move out of the flat, as I would be working on campus. I had grown attached to its bleakness. My orphan status assured the job, though I did not strictly need the money. But it was a good excuse for Mona, and most of all for Jamie. He would be devastated when he found out, but I knew he wouldn't get on with Jules anyway. It was best for me to stay here and for Jamie to get on with his life. I hoped he would hang out with boys his own age, even have a girlfriend someday. He could help George C out on the farm that he would eventually inherit. I didn't mention it to Mona on the phone. I saved it for the wedding.

The exams didn't go so well. My head a blur, my fingers slipping on the keyboard, not following the score. I watched out the window, onto the college courtyard, as students left with cardboard boxes. I did not see Mill among them.

Despite our plans, I was nervous about Jules coming back for the wedding, and so was Sandra. She gave him the money for the suit that he bought in a darkened shop in Camden. It had tails from the

1920s, and he bought a white shirt with ruffles. I liked it, but wondered what Mona would think. As the day of our departure grew closer, I worried about Jamie and what Jules would think of him.

19

We arrived on the bus from Dublin. We had come by overnight boat and coach like Jules wanted. I felt sticky and itchy all over and my bladder hurt. I had insisted that we weren't collected. So when we walked up to the house, everyone was busy. George C was putting up a picture in the hall of my parents. He beamed when he turned and saw us at the door, and my parents smiled out blankly behind him.

'When's the record coming out?' he said.

This had been his standard greeting for years. I hugged him and went through to the sitting room. I sat on the couch with Jules, who refused George's offer of tea. Jamie just stood and stared vacantly. Mona came rushing down the stairs.

'You are very welcome Julian. *Céad Míle Fáilte!*' Mona exclaimed, attempting to hug him after she hugged me. He stiffened and glared over her shoulder, mouthing to me to get her off him.

Mona was rushing around, as she was still at school and had little time to be the stand-in mother. I watched her from the couch as she rushed by, then got up to follow her. I noticed from behind her on the stairs that she had put on weight in the past six months. She had bought a hideous orange knitted suit, with a skirt that was all askew. It was meant to be it seemed, when I tried to straighten it. I told her it was gorgeous all the same.

'Jules is very nice,' she said, but I knew she didn't think that at all. She attempted to apply fake tan.

'I got a job for the summer at the college,' I said.

'Congratulations,' she replied.

I knew she was hurt, though. She took the mitt and went into the bathroom. I saw the long, silent summer stretch ahead for the three of them.

'Will Julian do something with his hair for tomorrow?' she called from the bathroom.

'He can't comb it out it for the wedding if that's what you mean.'

'Does he need to borrow a suit from George?'

'No, why?' I said curtly.

She came out and looked at me sharply.

'I won't be spoken to like that Marina,' she said, narrowing her eyes.

She went back in and locked the door. I went back downstairs.

When I sat back down beside Jules he didn't respond, and I knew he was in a dark mood.

'Don't leave me alone with that little freak again,' he whispered, too loud.

I winced as if he had slapped me.

'What's wrong with him anyway?'

'He has epilepsy,' I muttered.

'Apart from that?' he asked.

I felt torn but stayed with the two of them, neither of whom spoke. Even George C couldn't break the tension with idiotic jokes.

My sisters failed to notice. Despite their half-hearted offer I did not come up to Fionnuala's old room, where they were drinking Bacardi and Diet Coke. Jamie eventually shuffled away so I put on the television. It was EastEnders; it was like being at Sandra's.

George came in and stood behind the couch, doing some awkward shuffling.

'Will you be joining us for a pint at The Anchor?' he asked.

He had never asked before; I was excited at the thought of this grown-up activity, and thought of Jules' enthusiasm for the pub in Farringdon. It wasn't matched exactly, but Jules grunted a yes.

I switched off the television, avoiding Jules' eyes but knowing he was rolling them. He followed us anyway, and that was the only communication for the rest of the evening. He sat beside me, drinking pints of Guinness, and no one spoke much.

'How's the London girl?' said familiar faces, not stopping for an answer before moving on through the crowd, leaving us there in the corner with George, who wasn't drunk enough yet to talk, except for a brief, awkward attempt.

'How does the Guinness compare?' was aimed at the unresponsive Jules.

When my sisters came in with their friends, the noise level rose as they screeched in the other corner. Not as much as I imagined they had at the hen party two weeks before, in an obscure town down south. I had been invited but had been thankfully mid-exam, and they hadn't really cared. At least I had missed all the L-plates, plastic penises and printed T-shirts with Fionnuala's name written across in large letters. She had showed us them earlier: they were emblazoned with the words 'super slag', never to be worn again. A waste of chemical-laden cotton, laced with more dye than pension day at the hairdressers. Jules was horrified; he had thought of Ireland as the last bastion of simplicity, as near to the earth as you could get. The only hens he had imagined in a pub where the egg-laying kind.

The human hens filled the pub in on the gross details of their trip, between more Bacardi and Diet Cokes. Interspersed with kisses from local old ladies with crazy stories about our childhood and lots of 'if your mother was alive God rest her'. This inevitably led to drunken tears. Most of the stories they reminisced on seemed like dotage to me, and by the look on my sisters' faces I could tell the tears were getting tired. I was also privy to the latest gossip: they told me Fionnuala's locally-bred husband-to-be was a bad lot. He was only after her money and the house, which I had presumed was Mona's now. I was surprised to learn that it was in fact the sole property of my oldest sister. Luckily, Jules seemed to shut all this out. I meant to come clean to him about the money but I didn't want to be labelled as a bourgeois, as responsible for the destruction of the earth. I'd have to admit to hiding it, and I felt guilty. He and Sandra had had no money when his father had died.

As the night went on, everyone drank far too much and a fight broke out in the corner. I was told that this was a row that erupted weekly and had done for the last few hundred years, between the same two families. So at least Jules got an historical view of Ireland in conflict before we went home at one in the morning.

He was very drunk and not used to darkness, so he stumbled several times along the road. He became more and more angry with me after every pot hole, as if I had poured the water in and frozen it myself. Badly-mended roads were out of his range of experience, and quite the opposite of the pub-closing taxi or bus home experience, under the safe glow of the streetlights. We fought in whispers.

'Why were you ignoring me?' he hissed.

'I wasn't,' I said, shocked.

The key was in the door. I went and sat in the living room, my head blank with drink and the confusion of being at home, but with Jules. He went straight up the stairs; I heard him slump on the bed above me.

Jamie came downstairs and hugged me awkwardly, but said nothing. I wished we were young again and could go under the covers and escape, but we couldn't do that now.

20

My sister's wedding day arrived slowly throughout the night. Hairdryers, hairdressers and ironing boards using up half the national grid. I was changed, and had myself ready too early. Jules hadn't got up, and lay in the half-darkness of the bedroom. We were due at the church at 11.30 so I persuaded Jules to get up, in between Mona giving me funny looks.

She eventually said, 'For God's sake Marina, it's your sister's wedding. Isn't that why he's come all the way here.'

We walked to the church, getting soaked on the way; I knew this would annoy my sister immensely. Jules barely spoke, and I felt tense as we entered the church. I reluctantly brought him down to the front, where the family sat.

Of course, Jules knew nothing of the stand-up-sit-down-kneel-downs required. So he ignored them. I could feel the attention it was getting all over the chapel. Eyes were on him rather than on my sister. She was walked down the aisle by George C, he being the father substitute. She looked like a meringue. Her dress was creamy-white with puffy sleeves, and the skirt jutted out from her waist on each side. My other sister Rachel, the head bridesmaid, led a troupe of familiar faces in burgundy. Their flowers all coordinated, white and burgundy with sprays of green. I was relieved I had been left out. Fionnuala had relegated me to a lesser role. Mona had rung me after Easter to break it to me. She had sold it to me like I was still a child in school, saying that I would much prefer the new arrangements. She was right.

The church contained the entire human contents of the area that surrounded the four local pubs. We were related to most of the congregation and if we weren't, the groom was. The unwritten rule of local weddings is as follows: you can't not invite someone without releasing a feud that will carry itself into the pub for centuries to come. Luckily my sister was not short of cash, and had invited two hundred and fifty people for salmon or beef to the golf club. They would celebrate her wedding to the man she loved, or had settled for. She was twenty-nine now, and needed to get on with child bearing. It was time for a break from Dublin life.

The mass droned on, with dire readings and songs by their various school friends. I had avoided this fate; my part was to play piano at the hotel before the band arrived.

The flower arrangements were gaudy, and the smell of lilies overpowered the church. There was the inevitable rendition of *The Wind Beneath My Wings*, badly sung by the woman who always sang for local events. She was slightly out of tune, and got redder as she reached her impossibly high crescendo.

They exchanged their vows and came out of the church to throw the bouquet, which my other sister caught. Rachel had recently got engaged herself to another local, as ever distantly related. How they had both ended up with locals amused me, as they both had left here as fast as they could. They had barely come to see me after my parents died but had obviously been around. Just not near Mona or me. Maybe it was one of those quaint emigration stories about meeting the boy next door in the big smoke; I didn't ask. The reception gathered, and Jules got plunked on a table with a batch of the old ladies who were distant relatives of my father's. They were all from my father's neck of the woods, not too far away, but I'd not seen them since the funeral.

They ate the bland vol-au-vents as I began to play, shovelling them into their mouths from the silver platters held by local teenagers in black and white. The guests ate as if in sync with the music. Jules drank copiously from the trays of champagne. My distant aunts talked to Jules, who barely looked up, but that didn't deter them from asking questions. They supplied the video to my soundtrack as I imagined them rambling on about my dead mother, about how I looked like her when she was my age and so on.

Although she was much prettier really, and I'm sure they commented on this. It appeared Jules said nothing to defend me, and drank to drown out their sound and mine. As the crowd was seated, I joined them. A brief lull ensued, in time for the speeches. My sister's now-husband mentioned her deceased parents, and the wish that they were there. I played a concerto in my mind as his mouth moved to express his so-called sadness, and my sisters bobbed in tune. I knew Deborah and Jerome would have loved the chance to splash out and show off their money like this. To patronise their lowly distant kin, to remind them of how much money they had. Even after their death they could remind people of this.

The best man, who was Rachel's fiancé, then took over, and made jokes about the groom and bride's dubious sexual past. I was horrified to learn of the goings-on in this small town, but luckily everyone was too drunk already to do anything but laugh. Though I was sure that the information would be stored in the backs of their brains to be regurgitated another time, maybe when my sister wasn't paying for the drinks, with bits added in the meantime. Meanwhile, the bride and bridesmaids giggled wildly. I wasn't convinced, and went back to my inner soundtrack of the day, *Alkan's Preludes*. For some reason it seemed appropriate, the dull tones like a grey day at the beach.

The speeches rolled on, and I realized how little I knew about my sister. Apparently Fionnuala volunteered with special needs children in Dublin. She had been elected for the Students' Union when she was in college. I was relieved that I would not be prevailed upon to make a speech. The information did not inspire me to get to know them or their partners. It made me vow not to come back for Rachel's wedding, and as it turned out I didn't.

The speakers grew increasingly drunk. When it was George C's turn he could barely slur. Fionnuala whispered furiously, and I'm sure pledged anew to get him out of their rightful home. Mona cringed, and Jamie sat forlornly at the children's table like a zombie. The other children ignored him, and he was forced to endure the giggling directed at his father. I could only imagine what Jules thought of the whole thing, as his back was to me.

When the meal was over, I returned to the piano. The rest of the crowd stampeded to the bar, to order double and triple drinks in case the free bar ran out. I may as well have been piped-in music but I played on rather somberly. I drew a few liven-it-up remarks from winking men, and jokes about funerals. These jokes were shushed as inappropriate, considering our past. I couldn't remember the funeral much but I knew it had ended here, in the golf club. The décor was the same: cream walls, with a border of pink and brown paisley that matched the heavy pelmet curtains. The guests were much the same too, just slightly older. The cycle of life and death flowed as I played and forgot about Jules, and even Jamie. The wedding inspired what the exams could not.

Jamie was still at the children's table, left alone with the jelly and ice cream. The other children had disappeared; they were wired at this stage, full of fizzy drinks from the bar and sips of abandoned alcohol. The elderly aunts stored it all in their database as they looked on in horror.

The tables were soon moved, but left behind stray food remnants and torn tissue as they were dragged away from the floor. The sweep-up began in an operatic fashion. I remained distant from Jules' glowering mood and Jamie's growing bewilderment. Both of them stared and glared at me with equal intensity. Jules made the first move forward, and propped a drink on the piano lid as if to deter Jamie by an invisible force. He went to the bar again and again for more double gin and tonics. Knocking them back, he leant his elbow on the walnut swirl and shielded me from Jamie's need, enjoying a panoramic view while blocking mine. He had loosened his shirt, ditched his jacket and let his dreads down from the ponytail suggested originally by Sandra. As time went on he grew more hunched and sullen, then he moved to the bar. The band arrived and began to set up, as did the second-chance guests who had missed the dinner invite. I hadn't realised there could be so many people in anyone's life, and wondered what it would be like to know so many people. The band had now set up, and Rachel indicated that the first dance was about to begin. I ended my set and got up to no applause.

As I walked over to Jules, he got up. He grabbed my hand and dragged me towards the door. We ended up in the car park outside the kitchen; the door was propped open with an empty keg. It smelled of steam and dirty dishes. A girl I vaguely recognised was smoking outside. Her foot on the wall behind her, looking upwards.

'Could you not have stopped sooner? You left me there with those people asking me endless fucking questions,' he hissed into my face. His eyes were cold.

'Sorry, you know what weddings are like,' I said, startled by his venom.

'Really? This is what weddings are like? How the fuck would you know?'

'Sorry,' I said, looking down. I could not bear the deadness of his gaze.

'I agreed to come here with you to protect you and this is what I get? Fuck that Marina.'

I felt the lump in my throat dissolving into tears and swallowed hard.

'Sorry my house isn't as big as yours. My mother is still alive. Is that it? I'm supposed to feel sorry for you now?'

I shook my head, biting my lip and looking down at a weed struggling through the tarmac beneath my satin shoes.

'I'm not going back in there. Come on, we're going.'

He pulled my arms. The smoking girl looked over, threw her cigarette down and turned towards the kitchen.

Tina Turner's *Simply the Best* seeped out from the dancefloor.

I didn't ask him to go back for my wrap. We walked home in the half-dark and the fuming silence. I felt lost and spinning in the twilight as the midges attacked us. Jules marched ahead. I couldn't keep up in my heels. I went over my ankle in another pothole but welcomed the pain.

When we got back to the house, Jules erupted again in the darkness and insisted I ring the airline straight away. I managed to get a flight for the next day. He did not object to flying back. I wondered how I'd tell Mona and Jamie as we went up to the room and lay down in the dark. I stroked Jules' hair, trying to calm him down; he stayed turned away from me. I only got up when I heard the front door open. It was Mona and Jamie. She had come home to get him to bed and, I imagined, to get away from George C, who had probably got even drunker by now. I could well imagine him, dancing around, doing the conga. Being encouraged to do so by the laughing distant kin and locals, who relied on alcoholics for immediate entertainment and future gossip. This wedding would have to last until the next funeral. The stories of George were mounting, to his face with a laugh in the pub, half-prompted by himself, and then behind his back when he got too drunk. Of course, the best stories were reserved for disgruntled parents at the school, if Mona got too high and mighty for her blown-in boots. George stayed violence-free as long as he was not given vodka, whereupon he would fight and then cry in attrition. Sometimes, if the night was particularly boring, he would be slipped vodka via the barman, who'd laugh when he turned on someone and even egg him on further, before throwing him out. I imagined Mona had left before the inevitable.

She was surprised to see me come down the stairs as she had obviously expected me to still be there, still back at the golf club, catching up with the old school friends she seemed to think I possessed. Jamie was pleased to see me alone; he even raised a smile. The three of us sat up at the breakfast bar and had toast and cocoa, which Mona made us. It was like old times, when George C was out and we couldn't sleep, or had stayed up on a weekend to watch a late film. I couldn't break it to them that I was going in a matter of hours, and answered non-committal to any plans that were made. I tried to steer the conversation back to the wedding and the mad aunts, the band, anything to stop me having to tell them that I was going.

'Marina your piano was gorgeous. Everyone was talking about it.'

I smiled weakly but avoided her eyes.

'What is it Julian plays again?'

'The violin,' I told her for the tenth time.

'Well, there's a trad session in The Strand tomorrow night. He might like that. He might get inspiration.'

When I steered the conversation back to the wedding again she looked hurt.

I ended up leaving a note the following morning, taking advantage of the lie-ins. I woke Jules so we could catch the early bus to Dublin. Jamie saw me go past in the hall, and I stopped and waved. He stared over the quilt as if he'd been awake all night, and then covered his face.

We waited at the top of the road for the bus in the bleary silence. I worried that maybe Jamie would wake Mona, and that she would come driving after me and insist I return to the house. But the bus came, so we got on and sat down the back. I exhaled as it juddered off. Jules put his arm around me. He then stuck on his Walkman and looked out the window. I looked out and saw a Coke bottle top, competing with roadside poppies for brightness and symmetry. I tried to fill up my head with thoughts of the summer. I tried to listen to the unrealistically chirpy DJ talk between chart songs that were barely audible above the rattling and bumping of the bus and Jules' Walkman. I tried tuning out Jamie's face, staring from under the quilt in the half-light of the curtained room. Knowing I was leaving him to face Mona's disappointment with my departure and her imminent rows with George over his behaviour at the wedding. The return of my sisters to row over the house. The prospect of the summer with George C, and no solace from me.

21

Things settled into a routine. I saw Jules, the people I worked with, and Sandra on occasion. Jules hung around the campus if he wasn't at the Holland Park squat. I went upstairs to the flat for lunch, or occasionally I met Jules in the canteen. It had been renamed 'The Breeze Restaurant' for the summer visitors. Though the stifling heat of central London precluded any such notion. Abandoned by students, it took on a morose air. The college administration staff drank endless cups of coffee alongside the families of four, who had booked dorm rooms for sensible sightseeing holidays. Fathers in sandals silently fumed as their wives tried to persuade the children to eat the lumpy mashed potatoes and congealed pasta bake.

The reception was white and sterile, like the flats; it smelled of the used paperbacks that were kept behind the desk on a Formica white shelf. The manager, Gary, was not a student: he was from somewhere off the London map of England. Like most people, he thought I was a bit slow, and when he was out front he explained things to me. Obvious things. My eyes would glaze over, and he'd take it as incomprehension rather than disinterest on my part, then he'd leave me to it.

I checked the guests in and out without thinking. The Americans would ask me whereabouts in Ireland I was from.

'A small place you wouldn't have heard of,' I'd say, or 'my parents used to live in America before I was born,' to change the subject.

I only called Gary if there was a complaint about the rooms.

He spent most of his time playing solitaire in the office behind me, though on the rare occasions I came in he'd close it down guiltily. Sometimes I'd hear him talk to his girlfriend on the phone. He'd talk more than her, not like Jules and me. Jules dismissed him as 'one of them', the corporate drones who'd all be wiped off the face of the earth as they wouldn't know how to survive without a

McDonalds. He didn't see him as a threat.

I rang home less and less, and usually when I knew no one was in. Sometimes Mona would ring the reception desk. Jules walked me to and from the lobby on his way to daily meetings at Holland Park.

'Did the home grabber ring again?' he said, when he noticed that I was more silent than usual.

He made comments about Mona being a thief, and trying to win me away from my sister's side to hers over this whole house thing.

'That isn't what's going on,' I muttered.

He was convinced that it was all a callous plan of Mona's from day one. To move to a small town, marry a local man and kill off his nearest relations, who happened to have children, who would then be in need of a guardian.

'Well don't think I'm going to go back there again with you. And you know you'd be better off to stay out of it.'

I wearily tried to stand up for her, but it was easier not to.

The weeks went on. Jules and I sometimes practised together, occasionally watched foreign films at the old cinema, or visited the squat in Holland Park on my days off. The summer passed in the dead-still heat.

A new flat-mate moved in in second year. Caroline had returned after a year's exchange on the European programme. She had been in Barcelona, and talked of nothing else. She didn't seem bothered that Jules was always there, although she clearly did not like him, he said, but was rarely in anyhow. When she was there she spent long hours on the pay-phone in the hall, talking loudly in Spanish.

Sandra now shared Jules' view that I had been brought up by a wicked stepmother and two ugly sisters. Not to mention Jamie as Buttons and my Cinderella role, with Jules cast as Prince Charming. A white, British, only son, talented at music and nearly finished college.

'Wendy always says I'd have been better off sending him to Croydon College, saved myself a fortune,' she'd say.

'Probably be able to get a job out of it too.'

But then she'd acquiesce.

'But he was always ever so talented. I could hear it, even when his father would tell him to shut up. Drove him up the walls it did. Had to pay for the lessons myself.'

'I even brought him to a competition in Redhill the day after the funeral,' she'd add for effect.

She lived through him, her widowed civil servant existence quickened by the violin soundtrack that would culminate in his debut at the BBC's 'Last Night of the Proms'. I figured his sullen stance was genetic, as she told me his dad had been the same. I got the feeling she was glad he had died. She'd turn up the real flame gas fire when she talked about him, as if chilled by his very thought.

'Did I ever tell you Julian's father played the banjo?'

I had to suppress a giggle at that. I saw him in my mind, a grimacing George Formby singing about cleaning windows.

When I'd ask Jules about his dad, he'd just say that he protested because of him, because of how he died. But then he was silent.

I'd tell him about my parents to try to bridge the gap.

Once, when we were in an empty lecture hall doing assignments, I brought it up again. He leaned close to me. 'Can you shut the fuck up?' he hissed. 'I don't want to talk about my fucking Dad. He's dead like yours, OK? Eaten by worms who are probably dead from eating the crap that was in his body in the end.'

The tone of his voice was filled with the intense hate he usually reserved for Sandra. I felt tears welling up, but drew the water back. He began to gather up his stuff as if to go. I felt I was falling off a cliff. A steep fall into the air, sharp, cold air. Then loneliness bit and whistled through my centre, and I made to say something. He sat down at that point and rolled his eyes, but indicted that he'd stay. He sat, scribbling notes carefully while I pretended to stare at a book about Handel. I couldn't even focus on the pictures. I knew I had nowhere to go except the airport.

O'Hara wants to know why I stopped going to lectures. He says mental illness often increases in severity when young people go to college. He says he has spoken to the college. It is the first time he has admitted that he has spoken to others about me.

Sometimes Jules would say that he'd seen me flirting with lecturers or other students. I denied it all. I, who had lost some weight in first year, began to wear only leggings and baggy cardigans to hide myself. Then it became habit, as nothing else felt comfortable. Jules didn't like me to wear nice clothes, as he demanded to know whom I was trying to impress. He asked me where I thought they had been made, and by whom, and at what cost? I denied seeing anyone, or even wanting too, but it was no use. He made snide remarks when we were together about me looking at other men or boys. He often whispered between clenched teeth at me in the common room where I practised. My music began to suffer, as I was so busy trying not to look at anyone else or to attract attention that I could no longer get lost in it. I played stiffly and it began to show in my grades. I no longer progressed, but faltered on every note. He was like a judge at the *Feis* marking down the faults, decreasing the scores.

When I couldn't play anymore, I'd open the blue leather notebook; it was the only thing I had of my father's. I got it from him when I was seven, before he died. I used it to write in pieces that I had learned. I grouped them under composers, and wrote in key changes or places where I needed to improve. The entries declined over the months. I went to college less and less, though I longed for the solace of being lost in the notes, in the ivory. My piano was the only place I had to escape to before Jamie was born. I used my fingers to play Good King Wenceslas on the bedcover, my fingers dry and useless; I remembered Jamie's laughter.

Caroline tried to broach the topic one morning, when Jules had left. I was eating my breakfast. Strawberry Pop-Tarts and instant hot chocolate.

'Good band playing the SU tonight,' she said.

I didn't reply.

'Fancy coming? The Tiger Lilies, I think they're called.'

I shook my head, mouth full of Pop-Tart.

'How long have you been going out with Jules?'

'Over a year,' I said, swallowing my breakfast in a bid to answer.

'A night out without him would do you good. The Spanish have a saying about that, *ley pareja no es rigurosa* ... oh I can't remember what it is now...' she tailed off.

'Anyway, the gist of it is, what's good for the goose is good for the gander.'

I didn't know what she meant.

When I met Jules later he asked me to go to Croydon with him. I said I was going to get an early night and he left. The minute he was gone she came into my bedroom, smiling.

'Let's get some make-up on you,' she said. 'And I have the perfect dress!'

She dabbed at me with the make-up brush despite my protestations. I tried on two of her dresses, but settled for a T-shirt of hers over jeans.

The SU bar was packed. The support act were sound checking. After a few drinks, I couldn't remember why it had been so long since I'd been anywhere without Jules. My body began to subconsciously relax without him there, making nasty comments about the dubious talent of the band or accusing me of fancying the lead singer. The keyboard player was wearing a fedora; I tuned in to him. Could keyboards be my progression on from the piano, where I was stuck?

I danced in public, maybe for the first time since I had been out with Mill and we had frequented every student social gathering together at the beginning of first year. Before Jules. I wished she were here so I could talk to her.

I had begun to fantasise about Jules' death at a protest, crushed by the diggers he lay in front of. Just as I had fantasised about my parents, hoping they'd die on the way home from the golf club. I could see no other escape. I danced and I got drunker, tipping back the special-offer shots from test tubes that Caroline had suggested. I bought all the drinks for us.

'If I had known you were buying I would have eaten something before we came out,' she shouted, laughing above the music.

I drifted, remembered no more, as nothing mattered. I no longer knew about who I had been, who I was or wasn't looking at.

Then I knew I was looking at Jules.

22

Jules sat me on the bed, fully dressed, while I threw up into the washing-up basin. The vomit was purple and black, everything was spinning and then there was nothing again. When I woke up again it was early, and I wondered if I had died. The hollowed-out head that must have been mine was devoid of everything except a need for sugar. I gulped rank water from the tap in the bathroom then retched into the toilet, dizzy, falling onto my hands and knees. Jules loomed behind me but said nothing. I got up, wiping my mouth, and turned. He stepped aside as I stumbled back to bed with a sinking feeling, not remembering how I had got home, but I couldn't bear to ask. Jules stood at the bottom of the bed and just stared at me, as if how I felt inside had physically manifested itself upon my face. It was like he was staring directly into the bile in my stomach and the thumping in my head, my blood vessels turned inside out and pulsing like a mess from a B movie. He stared as if I revolted him, and I shut my eyes until he went out, slamming the door behind him.

I lay groaning until Caroline's head appeared around the door.

'Breakfast in the canteen?' she asked.

I shook my head. My stomach turned and spun at the thought.

'You were in a pretty bad way last night. He was here when I brought you back. I told him he'd need the basin,' she said, looking at it beside me, stained purple. The drummer was gone when I got back. You owe me now!'

I turned over onto my side.

She left, slamming the flat door behind her.

I lay in bed for two days, retching, until I could finally sip some water and eat some of the dry toast brought by her. Jules didn't come back, and my stomach lurched as I thought of how little I remembered.

The more he stayed away, the more I screamed out for him. I heard him on the stairs at every creak. I sat watching the door and longing for him to come, but fearing what he would say. I went back to college on the third day and hung around third-year lecture halls, but I didn't see him. There was no one to ask and I wondered had he committed suicide, as I had betrayed him by sneaking out without telling him. I imagined that he had been killed in a tragic rail crash on his way home. I scanned for such news anxiously in the newspapers in the library. There was nothing.

On the fourth day, I went to Croydon. I had waited until evening so Sandra would be in. When I rang the doorbell she answered, but was not her usual chirpy self. She sat down on the cream sofa without speaking, and it wasn't until she got up to put on the kettle that she said anything.

'You've got a nerve,' she said.

I went to the toilet and sat on the closed lid, staring at the door. It was as if I had eaten hundreds of Fizz Bombs. My hands were shaking, and I knew I'd made things worse by coming. I could hear Sandra crashing about in the kitchen. When I came back, so did she. She plunked a cup of tea in front of me, as if she couldn't break a sacred English tradition and let the royal family down by not making me a cup of tea. Despite what I'd done to her son.

Jules came downstairs. He stared at me, but then sat down as if nothing had changed. The casual observer, who, say, had been spying in the window for the last while, would think this was a normal suburban night in, but the atmosphere was not like that inside. It was the usual prime-time, over-enthusiastic-English-presenter TV. Sandra got up during the nine o'clock news.

'Well, I'll leave you two to it shall I. I'll be down the local if you need me,' she said in Jules' direction.

After she left we sat through the news, and still nothing was said. He turned as the weather began. I sat still and shook. He got up and sat beside me and went as if to kiss me, but just fumbled and groped. He did it right there on his mother's cream couch and he didn't wait. I kept thinking that it would soon be over, the tension and coldness and the pain. But I was numb and frozen as he then got up and resumed watching the television. I knew this was how Jamie felt after the fits. I had ignored him as Jules now ignored me. I stiffly got up to catch the last train.

'You can stay here,' he said.

'OK,' I said.

I was walking up the stairs when he shouted after me. 'And you can move out of that flat.'

I moved out of the flat the next day. I stuffed all my belongings in bin bags and into a taxi. I met Caroline when I was bringing down the second last load. She was stunned but scornful.

'Made you leave has he? So he can keep a closer eye on you?'

'24 Appian Crescent, South Croydon please,' I said to the driver.

The taxi driver asked to see the money before he agreed to drive so far. He didn't say a word after that. On the radio, the DJ announced a holiday competition to the Red Sea. I imagined ringing in and winning the holiday, and allowing Mona and Jamie to have my prize. Then they'd be happy, and send me a bright postcard with coral, fish and blue, clear sea, with not a hint of Palestinian oppression. The armed guard at the complex wouldn't be on the postcard; it would be just like a shopping trip to Belfast, but with sunshine. Just sun and sea and the distraction from what I had done. Abandoned them. Instead, with this dream holiday, they'd praise my generosity, and indeed Jules'.

I never rang in or entered the competition, though I had meant to when I got to Sandra's house. I knew Jules would object, and I didn't want to set him off. He'd start lecturing about Palestinian rights. I wished he would talk to his mother about all this, instead of dictating to me when something appeared on the television. He went blank when Sandra ranted. She'd purse her lips when she mentioned foreigners and gypsies, not that there were many in the white world of South Croydon. She was part of the brigade of dyed-blonde, permed-haired women, accompanied by tight-lipped, suited-and-booted men who kept the minorities beyond that point, and kept the rest of Surrey safe from dilution. The guardians of the trifle and custard. Living in their three-bed houses in neither London nor Surrey, with their coloured-shirted sons and shiny shoes and crop-topped daughters. With the occasional hippy like Jules to give them something to give out about when they were bored with foreigners and terrorists. My stay would provide some raised eyebrows. Some light, non-threatening relief to blame falling house prices on.

The taxi cost twenty-nine pounds, and I knew Jules wouldn't approve. I waited for my pound change, so the driver left the cases on the pavement and drove off. The exhaust's oily trace was left on my tongue.

O'Hara is fascinated by my move to the suburbs. He brings me back to it, again and again. I no longer know what parts I told him and what parts he gleaned from Jules and Sandra.

23

What had happened between Jules and I that night at the Students' Union was never discussed. I never heard his version of the events. I just moved into the box room at the top of the stairs. It was beside the bathroom, so I could hear all the bodily functions of the house. I didn't know why I was there. I stayed, though there was little room for my belongings and none for a piano.

On the first morning of the new regime I woke to the sound of Sandra banging about the kitchen. I checked Jules' room; it was empty. When I got into the kitchen, the Daily Mail was on the table and the coffee machine was filtering through. Sandra acknowledged me with a grunt from behind the ironing board.

I left her rent every week on the ironing board cover. Seventy pounds a week, as that's what my rent had been (although I had paid for the term in advance and had lost my money). Nothing was ever said about the rent, though she did seem to get her hair done more often. Dinner arrived at the same time every night, made by Sandra. We sat in silence to bland meals on trays in front of the television. I couldn't practise piano, just the violin. Although Jules practised and composed in his room most nights, he did not want us to duet anymore. He said he was working on something new. Sometimes I listened; it was a folk tune. It reminded me of Irish trad.

I began to watch television with the same intensity as Sandra, but usually on the portable I had bought in Argos for my room. On a Tuesday, when Sandra went out to her weekly aerobics class, I would go to his room and lie on his bed while he practised. Then it would happen.

I longed for tenderness, the tenderness that went into playing his violin. I watched his fingers caress the strings and the bow feather across them, making beautiful, ancient music. I watched his hands, knowing they were not capable of translating this tenderness, inflicting such symbiosis, onto a living thing. Wood and strings were pliable to him where my flesh was not.

After, we would lie on his single bed. I would talk and talk about nothing, and he would listen but say nothing. I knew he was angry with me for getting drunk, and I presumed I had done something awful but dared not ask what. I thought of George C and the things he did and didn't remember after a night out. Jules' fuming reminded me of Mona's. So it seemed right that I was being made suffer. I talked about us moving out and getting a flat, or even a house. I supposed that when he forgave me it would happen.

His father's tenth anniversary loomed. Sandra had planned an anniversary dinner for relatives and friends in a nearby hotel. It was like my sister's wedding all over again, menus, seating plans, outfits and flowers. I hadn't thought they would care about such things, but it seemed they did. Even though Sandra had of late joined a dating agency. I knew this as they had rung when she was out. I had answered the call as I was waiting for my piano lecturer to ring me, regarding an appointment about my sliding performance. I knew a serious chat was in order; I had been late with assignments since I had moved, and often missed the whole week.

Even when I went in, I would just sit the same corner of the canteen in the half-light and eat alone. I watched as the other students kissed, drank, ate and sometimes threw food at one another, laughing. Jules and I would meet to walk down to the tube to get to the train before the big commuter rush. Then we wouldn't have to stand in the crammed aisles as far as Victoria before we could get a seat. I'd watch the lights along the tracks and look at us in the reflection of the windows. I'd read the ads over and over, for things I seemed never to want but pretended to be infinitely interested in. It stopped me looking at other people or directly at Jules.

24

I meant to ring Mona and tell her of my change of address, but Sandra made it clear that I was not to use the phone by buying one of those phone locks. She only took it off for her weekly conversations with her mother. About the ungrateful immigrant youths who were rioting in Bradford.

'Thugs the lot of them, they should be rounded up on a cattle truck and sent back to where they came from. I suppose we'll be safe with Marina here though, she'd get the IRA after them. Oh, I shouldn't joke. The Muslims will be bombing us next. Riot first, then the bombs, just like Ireland.'

She then went on to talk about Eric Cantona; she had seen him being brought into court in Croydon last week on her way home from work. 'Bloody Frogs,' she said.

I tried to study but it all seemed hopeless, the required information mounting like a rotting pile over my head. Lectures that I did attend made no sense; the words blurred in my head, jumbling like late-onset dyslexia. My brain felt like jelly, and I listened to it vibrate uselessly. One night I realised the hum was the Hail Mary. It went over and over in my head like a mantra. I started muttering along with it, over and over; it filled up the long, hateful silences that were lunchtime and the train home and the house in Croydon. Where forgiveness had been forgotten, and my unspoken crime magnified by their silence.

Jules pinched my hips one Tuesday night on the bed. 'Lay off the Fruit Pastilles or you'll be more horse than seahorse,' he said.

I never talked about it anymore; I had told Jules, but he did not choose to join me in the magnified darkness under the quilt, the warm, all-enveloping darkness.

I filled my head with bland trivia, other people's problems on the television; I watched the England fans rioting in Ireland at the football.

Then I'd switch off the volume and mutter into the silence and ask Virgin Mary to forgive me, to rescue me. I'd pray that she'd send Mona to bring me home. I saw she was angry that I did not know the joyful mysteries of the rosary, which Mona had knelt us down together to say on occasion. The endless prayers that I had half-muttered along to, kneeling over the back of the sofa. I had learned them at school too, but all I could remember now was *The Agony in the Garden*. I imagined a garden full of pillars and ivy like the hanging gardens of Babylon, like the conservatory in the first house we lived in. I knew how lonely Jesus must have felt then, abandoned and betrayed. I knew that, like him, I was free to go, but I didn't.

Many would see my situation as idyllic, O'Hara says. I imagine envious refugees stuck between borders in white tents, their children wearing old seventies jumpers. They would kill for a place like Sandra's.

I was treading frozen water, trapped, waiting for them to forgive me and end all of this. There was nowhere else to go except Ireland, and that seemed impossible. I knew that Mona and Jamie and George would now have left my family home. I imagined how disappointed Mona would be if I gave up on college. Gave up on the piano that had brought us together. That had brought Jamie back to me. I thought she and George must have returned to the tiny dormer they had built when they got married.

There was no solution that seemed tangible. I came to understand that I was being belatedly punished for killing my parents and for betraying Jamie. It was the only thing that made sense. I prayed incessantly for forgiveness, but accepted the punishment I was being given. I went to confession one day in an empty church near the college. I told the priest my sins.

'Bless me father for I have sinned. It's been two years since my last confession,' I said through the grille. 'I have lied and cheated, I have lost faith in God.'

He seemed unimpressed, maybe used to hearing about stabbings and drug dealing in the inner-city blocks. He wasn't even Irish, as I had thought all priests were, well the Catholic ones anyway. He gave me more Hail Marys.

I took the penance that had been handed down, and muttered it numbly back and forth to London on the train. I was waiting for the onset of the second-year exams, where all would be discovered and a lobotomy would be recommended and all the pretending would end. Fear thudded in my chest, telling me that if I let it out it would unleash a vacuum that would destroy me and take Croydon too. It would suck all the three-bed semis into the ground and shatter all the windows, like an unexploded IRA bomb from the eighties. Maybe Sandra was right; I was a terrorist.

In my dreams, I swam with Jamie. I woke up gasping the air of the dry central heating. It was always on. Its low, menacing buzz permeating the house from the gas boiler in the kitchen, despite Jules admonishment and warnings about global warming. I opened a window when it got too unbearable. My room, that was my dungeon, had been decorated many years before and belied the cream of the rest of the house with purple and gold borders and ruffles. I lost myself in them and used the flower patterns to count my prayers. Sometimes to tune out Sandra loudly asking Jules when I was going to leave. The answer to which he'd mutter, and then they'd talk in low whispers.

I went to see the doctor in the college, in the prefabs out the back by the canteen. I tried to tell her how I felt, but she saw it as homesickness. I was swimming through sludge, but she said I was depressed and prescribed me some tablets. I came back two weeks later and she wrote me a note to defer my exams. The tablets wiped out my religious visions of Mary watching from above. I felt lonely now too, as well as relieved; they sliced through the fog in my vision.

It was as though the condensation had been wiped to reveal a view. The view was cloudy.

O'Hara thinks I should try going to mass on Sunday. It is held here in the building. He thinks it will bring me comfort. He says he wouldn't suggest it if I wasn't making progress. It is to be my reward. I am to be rewarded by mass here, and in turn in heaven.

As Jules did his final exams, I started work again in the college. I went in and out on the train to a schedule, feeling comfortably numb. Watching the grey cloud that surrounded me from behind the glass. Whereas before it was as though it would swallow me up, now it was just there. Part of the landscape. Still blocking any sight or glimpse I might have of the future. Just me behind the reception desk.

There was a new manager this year, a woman. She paid me little attention and left me to it. She saved her wrath for the immigrant cleaners who changed weekly.

I took to reading the glue-filled bad English of detective novels. Instead of going to the library, I borrowed out of the selection we kept on the reception desk for the rainy days of the budget-constrained guests. All the plots were fairly similar. I would guess 'whodunit' quite soon into the foray, but would become fascinated by the endless catalogue of murders that seemed to be filling the area outside London. In these sleepy villages that I had never actually seen, but imagined to be totally different to the villages of Ireland from where I had come. I imagined that they would all have a village square with hanging baskets of red geraniums, matching the red brick houses and quaint Tudor pubs called after ancient royals. All filled with country squires who lurked murderously.

So my summer went, travelling around England in my head. I only rang home once. Fionnuala answered.

'Oh Marina how are you?'

The reality of Mona's move really hit me. I was shocked into silence.

'Mona moved into that new estate near the school. Briar Heights. Do you want her new number?'

She put down the phone and I heard her tend to the baby, who gooed contently.

'I'm pregnant again!' she said, after she'd given me the number.

'Congratulations,' I said, and put the phone down.

I rang the new number. No one answered. I didn't leave a message.

I couldn't imagine an estate in a village. I reckoned this would reduce the detective novel rate. The genre didn't suit such mod-con houses. They needed old mills and woods, the likes of which were disappearing as fast as the ubiquitous pavement was appearing beside street-lighted, landscaped gardens. There were fewer and fewer places where a body could be dumped, which someone could then find when out walking the dog. New shrubs hadn't the same power to disguise bodies, and it would be harder to be chased around a new estate by a soon-to-be-discovered villain. No old rivalries or torn love affairs would survive to provide motives for these crimes, in these Legoland places called after plants and trees.

O'Hara asks why I didn't tell Mona about what had happened. I didn't know how to explain it to myself. He asks me to explain why I felt trapped in a three-bed semi in Croydon, when I was free to come and go as I pleased? He asks me to explain what I mean by the isolation in the decreasing prayers? He asks me to explain a boyfriend who never forgave me for something that I didn't remember? The mother of the boyfriend who I insist didn't want me there, but who didn't insist that I go? A boyfriend who I tell him didn't talk to me, who pulled my hair in lieu of affection and who I say stared at me, and talked to his mother about me in disgust as if I was not there? And how I sat and took it all because I say I could not walk back to where I left Jamie shaking on the road?

All I wanted then was for Mona to know it all by my silence, and ask me to come home. To come back to live with them in their new house. I wondered if my mother had lived would she have guessed. Would she have even cared? Would I have told her, or would it have happened at all? The twists of paths of fate seemed like a mountain goat's trail, where I was perched at a bend and Mona stood far below, like a speck of grass. Surely there was a bedroom there, a spare one for me, why else did they get a four-bedroom house? I wanted to reach through the phone and pull myself through it. She would make me cocoa and sit me down; I could tell her what I had done.

But I had made my choice the year before, at the wedding. I had chosen Jules. I had made my bed so I lay in it, comatose. The pictures of my childhood stored in my head were fading. My childhood seemed like a set of negatives left out in the sun, just random images of the countryside, of obscure groups of trees and of views from the window of my first concrete home.

I tried the number again.

'Hello, it's me,' I said when she answered.

'Oh,' she said.

'How's Jamie?' I asked.

'Much the same.'

'How's the new house?'

'Very modern.'

'How's the school?'

'Same as ever, how's college?'

'Fine,' I lied.

'How's Julian?'

'Good,' I said.

She could have been a guest at the reception desk.

I tell O'Hara about this phone call one day in his office. It seems harmless and mundane to me. He extracts an hour's session from it.

The rock that Jules had placed in my throat, not on my finger like Mona would have wanted for me, dropped deeper when she put down the phone. I was left holding the receiver, feeling the sound echo and reverberate. I couldn't even cry. I knew now that my escape route was closed; I had the money but nowhere to go, no one to go there with. I tried to pray again but the words got jumbled, so I looked for a sign instead. I took stock of every magpie and black cat that crossed my path. I crossed my fingers, twirling and spitting for the single magpies. The answers I saw only enforced the dreadful feeling that something bad was going to happen, but with it the relief that something had to happen soon.

One Friday, Jules made an unexpected visit to the reception desk. I was checking someone in. 'I'm going to Newbury for a few days,' he said. 'Mark's taking the van.'

Other protestors had started living in treehouses to stop the huge bypass that was being built through a mature forest. It was the old Twyford Downs protest crowd gathering again; some of the older eco warriors who passed through Holland Park had told them about it.

'Mum's expecting you.'

I nodded and continued with the booking.

When he turned and walked away, I dreamed of murdering Sandra in his absence. In the latest book I had read, the villain had poisoned her lover's mother as the mother had disapproved of their relationship, but the villain had never been found out. Well not yet anyway, though I was sure she'd have her comeuppance. I reckoned there was nothing to lose now; life couldn't get any worse. It was Sandra who had come between us, with her seeping, passive malice that was too much for this world. She hated everyone and everything, and had infected Jules with her hate for me. Even though it seemed he hated her as much as me.

The gory pushing-her-down-the-stairs-and-burying-her-under-the-foundations thing seemed too obvious, but there were endless other ways that people were murdered in the books and on television every night. The books I had been reading never featured a peaceful way to shut someone up, but with her dead I imagined I could come alive again, practise my piano and pass my repeat exams and stop reading detective novels.

Further research was required so I went to the library that lunchtime, but didn't really know where to begin. Flicking through some literary fiction revealed nothing, and I didn't know where else to look. There was no 'How to kill your boyfriend's mother' section. The International Studies section was next; I considered trying to make her read some, especially some with a political message, that would kill her for sure. The hitman option was another TV-inspired possibility. Then Jules and I could sort out our differences like Jane and Rochester. The mad wife in the attic, who had to be Sandra, would die. Then I remembered that I had read an article in the Guardian magazine about India, where femicide was commonplace. I picked up some books on India, checked them out, and returned to my desk. Maybe, I reckoned, the books themselves might kill Sandra, shuffling upstairs in the night and congregating on her bed. I imagined her terror as she breathed for the last time, books flying at her like a horror film, her last breath cursing my name. These flights of fantasy would have to be enough to keep me sane for the weekend, I decided. I took the books home on the train.

O'Hara says I wanted to kill her so that Jules would be an orphan like me. He says I tried to kill her because I believed I had killed my parents. If I had killed her, I would have been punished for all three deaths.

The house was still empty when I got back. I went to my room and sat on the bed with my coat still on, and began reading the book about India. Buddhism sounded just like Catholicism but they had mantras instead of prayers, and rebirth instead of heaven. There was an elaborate diagram of the Buddhist wheel of life. Turning the book around in my hands, I noticed the human beings were near the top of the wheel, almost in Nirvana. Human misery was all I could see. All on the wheel, all of us crammed in, everyone I knew. Sandra every day miserable because her beloved England was going to hell in a handcart packed with foreigners, gypsies and Irish wife beaters. Jules was miserable too, because I had betrayed him, because I didn't love him the way he loved me, because the corporations were destroying the world, and because we were being poisoned but no one else seemed to care. I was unhappy because I thought the opposite, and Mona was unhappy because of George C's drinking. Jamie was unhappy because I had left him alone.

Then I saw Jamie again, staring at me from under the bedclothes when I called Jules the morning after the wedding. I couldn't bear it. I had thought about writing to him, but didn't know what to say. How could I have explained it all? Why I had left him for London, why I had chosen my piano over him. Maybe I had killed him, but tried to console myself by pretending he would be better off. He might be happier hanging around without me, his plump, orphaned cousin, who was seven years older and had no friends. Maybe, when I left, he had made friends and begun to fit in. Maybe he had joined the GAA club. I imagined his red hair streaking across the midday pitch, hurl in hand, with George cheering him on. This was mere fantasy. I had made my choice, all I had now was Jules, and so I had to get him back from Sandra. Despairing again, I returned to the books, looking as to how they got rid of troublesome females. Then I heard the door slam shut and I jumped. I had been lost in a dream of Sandra, prostrate on a funeral pyre with her dead husband in remotest India, by the Ganges. People stared in wonderment, and

I imagined her yellow peroxide perm being the last thing to go.

Its halo surviving the flames and floating up into the ashes like a bad wig.

Sandra is the subject of one of O'Hara's sessions. He gets an hour out of her. I could give him ten hours if he wanted.

25

I felt too guilty to go downstairs. So I switched on the portable telly in my room. They were talking about Rosemary West's trial. Sandra came up the stairs, tapping on the door before entering.

'I suppose you'll be wanting your dinner?' she said in an accusatory fashion.

'Thanks Sandra, but I've eaten already,' I lied.

'Good, because I thought you'd be off with Julian, so I didn't get anything in.'

I didn't answer.

'Just you and me then for the weekend,' she said.

Edged with panic now, I moved to hide the book from her view. Even if it didn't reveal my thoughts of her imminent mortality it made me nervous, as I did not want her here for an hour in a rant about 'them all having to wear scarves'. I had heard that one before. People from Asia were savages, cannibals and heathens in her eyes. I began to scratch my arms nervously and she stared for a while, then pursed her lips, muttering to herself. She withdrew from the cell and shut the door, like a perfect prison officer. Probably wishing she could install a grille to look through.

The five o'clock news came on, and I remembered what Jules' friends had said about a girl from the animal protests who had been killed at Heathrow, that it was never on the news, but now the Newbury protest was the second item. I wondered if the protesters would be pleased. I tuned out again as heard the slurp of the freezer door opening: Sandra in search of a Marks and Spencer's meal for one, to eat in front of whatever soaps were on. Not for the first time, I thought of climbing out the window and down the drainpipe. Through I could just as easily have walked out the front door. Sandra would use the tiny under-stairs toilet, and not come upstairs again until she had woken up in the early hours. She'd fall asleep after her bottle of wine in front of the telly in her chair, to the late-night film that she always got excited about but never seemed to watch right through.

Suddenly, Jules' absence pervaded the house; it made me put down the book and tiptoe into his room. It was dark and smelled of sweat. Posters of bands adorned the walls. I got into his bed and lay down, smelling his pillow, and reached for that feeling of pureness that I could never summon when he was around. I lay staring at the posters on the wall. His wardrobe door was open, revealing his usual display of New Model Army T-shirts and combat trousers. Curious, I got up and poked around on the top shelf. I found a stack of tattoo magazines behind the piles of eco warrior leaflets and magazines. I took them down and flicked through, in fascination and disgust. Close-ups of intricate designs, compelling yet repellent, and the girls beneath the tattoos pouting for the camera, eyebrows and noses pierced. So removed from me in their skin-tight clothes and long, patent thigh boots. They looked unreal, like cartoon boots, the heels spiked and unworkable, but they explained Jules' lack of interest in me. I imagined myself in one of the magazines, in a black cat suit bulging at the zips. I shoved the girls back and tried to cover my trail, but guessed I could blame it on Sandra anyhow. I poked around some more but found nothing else that intrigued me. Then I must have fallen asleep, as I was awoken by Sandra's hungover ascent. I considered pushing her down the stairs but dismissed it as too messy, and not guaranteed to end in death.

I waited until she was settled and went back to my own room. The TV still flickered, a late-night talk show. The fall of Diana Spencer was the subject as usual, the antithesis to the tattoo girls. I switched it off and got back into bed, but couldn't get back to sleep. The images of those black-eyed women flipped over and over in my head, like a slide show with a faulty off button, until I put back on the light. I took my book downstairs to the kitchen and went to the fridge. In the yellow light of the fridge I found a chicken leg and ate it, as if to spite Jules. I turned back to the wheel of life, progressing from insect to fish to animal to human to heaven, and I wondered where in the cycle I would end up if I did go through with killing Sandra. I made a cup of soup and balanced it on the book, trying to stop it slopping. I sat up drinking it in the dark, the images of tattooed girls still turning over in my mind.

My dreams were dark and without respite all through the night; it was like I still awake. I dreamt that I was watching Jules and Sandra from up on a ceiling where I was tied up. Then I was back in Ireland and Jamie was tied up too. I tried to untie him but I couldn't. He looked at me, his face twisting and growing paler by the minute, then faded. Then I was back with Sandra and Jules, and he screamed and I tried to shout at her but I couldn't hear the words and there were planets spinning by me, making me feel dizzy.

I woke up feeling groggy and frightened, as I knew something had woken me up. It was a loud crashing sound, and then I heard it again. It was coming from downstairs. Sandra's legs were sticking out from under the kitchen sink, surrounded by pots, pans, oven trays, dusters and Brasso.

'Right, it's spring clean time so you can do your bit, you do live here,' she said.

With that she handed me a noxious cloth with a bottle of Brasso and told me to do the letterbox.

'God knows, let's get it done before Julian comes back or he'll start going on about us wasting water.'

'I'll just go and get dressed,' I mumbled.

I turned heel, wishing I had thought of a way to kill her the night before to avoid this on my day off. A precious Saturday in the suburbs of London. I had planned to persuade Jules to go to Brighton, and winced when I thought of him at the protests. I didn't wish I was there; I hated the thought of the crowds, and didn't see the point of trying to hold back what was inevitable.

I got dressed and ate a bowl of cornflakes under Sandra's tutting, as she scoured baking trays that she never used. The smell of the cloth took me back to my childhood, Jamie and me playing hide and seek under the stairs where the Brasso filled the dark cupboard with fumes, so when you were found you'd have lost all concept of time and space. However, this morning, combined with the bad dream and the forbidden chicken, it just made me retch. I ran into the garden and retched into a small conifer bush on my hands and knees. Sandra came out to see what was going on. She half-dragged me in and slammed the door shut, knocking the Brasso over, the oval spread of its yellow cream creeping towards the duster.

'Are you pregnant?' she hissed. 'Cause that's all I need, it's bad enough having you here without a little Irish bastard screeching. I suppose I'd have to look after it and my Julian would have to keep you here. Well I don't care what your religion says, you're having an abortion even if I have to give it to you myself.'

I tried to tell her that it was the chicken, but didn't have the strength after throwing up. I was trembling. She kept shouting.

'I'm bringing you to the surgery right now; we'll say it's an emergency.'

She forced my coat on me like you would a small child, and I followed her out of the house. She paused only to grab her bag off the hallstand, where it lived. I followed her into her immaculate 3-door hatchback and sat, unable to speak, a tear rolling down my face. She reversed out of the drive, nearly hitting the pillar, and took off jerkily down to the shopping centre, where the surgery was. It was full of Saturday shoppers. She drove round and round the car park, swearing, though I had seen her park there many times myself. She got out of the car after parking badly on the far side and I followed at her rear, dodging cars who were looking for parking spaces and not about to let human beings get in the way. She pushed through the surgery doors and marched up to the receptionist.

'It's an emergency,' she insisted. 'We need to be seen straight away.'

She gave only her own name before sitting down and flicking rapidly through a torn magazine. Each flick like a gunshot, reading nothing. I stared at the children's toys on the floor, a dirty cloth book and a seventies Fisher Price activity centre. I couldn't help leaning over to spin the psychedelic wheel, with pink vertical lines that wavered magically as it spun. Then Sandra spun her face to me and glowered, so I picked up a Reader's Digest and tried to read the page fillers and the not-so-funny anecdotes. I was in a numb haze, trying to act like being here was perfectly normal.

The doctor's door had a dark wood veneer, and when our turn came Sandra pushed me through it. The doctor was looking down writing, but when he noticed there were two of us he looked up through the top of his glasses. Before he could speak, Sandra did.

'I want you to do a pregnancy test, this girl is my son's girlfriend, she's Irish, and I think she's gone and got herself pregnant.'

I thought he'd ask us both to explain ourselves, but instead he calmly asked Sandra to leave. Well, he called her Mrs. Spoors. He was polite but firm. After rushing here on whatever build-up of rage she seemed somewhat deflated, and turned and left without protest. I could make out that she was outside the door. Dr. Wells got up, went to the door and opened it slightly.

'Mrs. Spoors, if you could go back to the waiting room please I would very much appreciate it.'

I heard her click back down the halls.

'Now young lady,' he said, 'How have you incurred the wrath of your mother-in-law? Were you caught in the act so to speak?'

I didn't speak.

'I expect you're on the pill aren't you, a sensible young lady like yourself? Girls usually are, well in advance of meeting the in-laws-to-be.'

A tear slid down my cheek as I tried to nod, but with it released a flood of tears that I had been storing up for months. I shook and even retched again, trying to speak, but the words stuck in my tonsils.

Dr. Wells looked calm as ever, and I guessed things like this happened to him all the time. He reached for some man-size tissues that were branded with the name of some hideous sounding drug and held them out. He asked me to tell him what the matter was.

All I could say was 'I want to go home,' because that was all I wanted at that precise moment. I suppose most people would say that they wanted their mothers at such times but I didn't have one, unless you counted Mona, and I had never been encouraged to call her so. The Brasso-fuelled memory of Jamie and I hiding in the dark cupboard was all around me, and seemed so far removed from the realms of this clinically bright, disinfectant-smelling doctor's office, thousands of miles across the sea.

'Well are you pregnant?' he asked. I shook my head and he smiled briefly, then dropped back to his normal expression. He pressed the speaker button and told reception to send Sandra up. She knocked and peeked around the door, almost timidly. He motioned for her to sit down.

'Now I know, Mrs. Spoors, it's hard to see one's son being taken away by another. Young people are sensible these days, much more than we were I fear, and this girl isn't pregnant, just a bit anxious. Now let's leave it at that, and I want to see you two put this behind you. What would the man in question think of having his favourite two ladies fighting over him?'

Sandra thanked him in a way that frightened me. I followed her like a bold child into the car, where we sat in silence.

'Let's forget about this little incident shall we?' she said before starting the engine.

She abruptly shoved the gear stick, grating and crunching into reverse, and nearly ran into a jeep in the process. I wished she had gone straight into it, and imagined the impact and the sweet feeling of pain. Imagined the glass shards slicing through my forehead in an effort to distract myself from the situation. To anesthetize me from the present, which had never seemed so clear and raw since the day I was born into this horrible grey life.

My murder fantasies ended at that moment. I realised she'd come back anyway to torment me. If I killed her now, the doctor would be witness to what had happened in the surgery that afternoon. He had obviously seen the murderous intent in my Irish terrorist eyes, and I imagined he was probably on the phone to the police already.

I could see the whole courtroom sequence now: in his report, he could give evidence of how it was clearly not self-defence. In the courtroom reconstruction Jules was sitting in the back benches, or in the balcony like in *To Kill a Mocking Bird*, silently wishing for a not-guilty plea but loving me anyhow.

Before the imaginary jury gave its verdict, we were back at the house, and she walked in front of me, past the overturned Brasso. She returned to the kitchen and switched on the radio, a dreadful country music show, as if nothing had happened. How she would hate the similarities she had with her Irish housewife counterparts. She picked up her cleaning without comment. I returned to my room and began to pack for the hundredth time. It seemed insurmountable, but I decided I'd tell Jules what had happened. I'd wait for him to come back and I'd tell him everything, and demand that we move back into the college residences. Or even into a swanky loft in North London. Or we'd go travelling, protest to protest, around Britain, in a bender like he wanted. I didn't care. I knew that I had to get us out of this suburban hell and away from the volatile Sandra before I lost my mind. I should have been studying for my ever-impending exams but I was still shaking from the vomiting and the ordeal.

I switched on the television. Right on cue there was an old black and white film beginning on Channel 4, replete with shocked ladies in ball gowns and good and bad men trying to respectively outdo them or be their undoing. It was unclear why they were doing this and to what end, but slowly my mind uncoiled from the ordeal that it had witnessed.

The calm didn't last. The horrible tattooed women jostled for my attention, away from the ringleted ladies in long dresses who swished around the screen. I tried to fight the scantily clad ladies, chasing them back into Jules' wardrobe and locking the door on them in my mind. But with the effort my stomach turned again, and I ran out the door and spewed in the hall on my hands and knees. My head was like a fuzzy television reception, the spots joining and rejoining like a kid's dot-to-dot puzzle composed by someone on LSD. I was dizzy, but crawled into the bathroom, got a washcloth from the stack in the basket, and crawled back to wipe up the sick. I prayed that Sandra wouldn't notice it. I crawled back into the room and lay on the floor behind the door. I wished for the sea to pour through the window and swallow me. I lay there until it got dark, then I dragged myself onto the bed and lay staring at the window, waiting.

Because then it dawned on me that I couldn't remember the last time I had had my period.

I am tempted to tell O'Hara about the doctor's appointment. He seems to have missed this visit in his files. Even if he has been speaking to Sandra, she wouldn't have told him about it. His detective skills are lacking, and I am lulling him into a false sense of security. I am getting better, he says.

I dreamt all night of Jules. My dreams were purple and violet, but I woke bright and early at dawn. When I got out of bed my head hurt, so I went downstairs for water; there was no sign of Sandra. I imagined she had drank too much and would be in bed for a while. I left the house. I was woozy in the sunshine but it was a sunny, hot June Sunday. Everything seemed to have an edge of beauty, even the yellowed grass and the smoggy air.

26

That's the thing I loved best about London, the parks full of trees and ponds and flowers that were all kept beautifully clean. Not a farmer or a herd of cows in sight. Jules said it was man's attempt to tame the wilderness. He hated parks; he said they were corporate scum's attempt to pacify us.

I lay back on the bench, blissed on anonymity, and looked at the sky. The birds drifted around in the blue. I imagined the joy of flight, and I thought about how easy life was for birds. They could just find a partner, build a nest and lay eggs. No Sandra on their back, accusing them hysterically of pregnancy and marching them off to a doctor. The thought of it made me laugh for the first time in ages, and I felt a ripple of warmth in my chest. I felt myself soaring with enlightenment and awe at the thought of becoming a bird. All those human female worries like rape, infertility, abortion and body image, all covered up forever in black feathers. To fly far away through the sky, far from where I came, and never to be thought of again. Their chicks grew up fast, then they were gone, then they'd have some more. Then I wondered how birds had sex, amid the flying and the feathers.

The warmth in my breath was snuffed out when I thought of him returning. I sat up and tried to immerse myself back in the book about India. I was no longer looking for ways to kill, just a way to live, because I knew there had to be change. Though I knew I was still being punished for what I had done to Jamie, and I could not go back to Ireland until I was ready. I had to get used to the black pit of despair that I had tumbled into like a medieval bear in the woods.

I realised that my exams didn't really matter, nor did the music.

I tried to picture myself as an oasis of calm in the centre of the urban South East, in the heart of industrialised Britain and the evils of consumerism. The very place where a new focus for the whole world could be if we worshipped and coveted the lives of fish, animals, and even plankton. I realized then that the world could be saved from the evils of pollution and meat consumption and inequity and animal exploitation, and we could all be calmer. The water would not come. If I really was pregnant we could bring up the baby in this floating world to be happy, to understand its purpose in life, to belong to all this beauty.

So I got up from the yellow grass, baked dry by weeks of sun, and walked back to the house, almost wishing in a way for a church to go into. Then I hit the edge of the dual carriageway beside the estate. Cars packed with unhappy children and adults crawled by, going to Ikea and other large warehouse shops filled with things they didn't need and that were designed to make them miserable.

Sandra was cleaning again and even feigned a smiling acknowledgement when I came back in. I went into the sitting room and sat down. She eyed me nervously as I did not usually come in unless Jules was there, but rather went straight to my room. She continued on with her dusting but I could see I was affecting her just sitting there. I tried not to feel smug, but to concentrate on the book. She went outside to put the duster back and I longed to go under there with it, under the stairs, and lock myself in. Meditate until I saw a clear way out. My brightly-lit faith was fading in the cream surround, amid her energy and the waiting for Jules' return. Sandra had gone out to her postage stamp garden. I followed her.

She jumped out of her skin when I sat on the back-door steps and began to read again. She rubbed on the factor-two bronzer and settled uneasily to sunbathing on her lounger. I read on; she did not comment on the book although I dared her to, not that she could see the title in the strong, airless light. She did not comment on anything for a change. I was unsure if this was plain and unadulterated sun-worshipping, or a ploy on her part to make up for yesterday's events.

Today is the first day of the rest of your life, I thought, and the sun exploded in my brain, and the dark reaches of my life in Croydon seemed to be wiped away.

We lay out in the sun until evening, half-asleep and agreeable for once, though Sandra shifted uncomfortably throughout the day in her sun lounger. I drank water all day, going in and out to the water filter in the fridge and avoiding the usual pitfalls of chemical-laden sugar-free squash that swelled me into oblivion. I didn't eat at all, not even when she offered a Marks and Spencer's prepared veggie lasagna and oven chips.

I didn't join her in front of the Sunday night drama, but wondered when Jules would get back. The urban heat had stifled my bedroom, so I lay down and fell asleep quite quickly.

When I heard the key blunted against the door I startled awake. It was Jules, crawling through the door. It was five a.m. on the square red numerals of the clock radio. I went to the top of the stairs and saw that he had knocked Sandra's handbag off the hallstand. I rushed down to pick it up, to maintain the harmony. As I rose, his twisted face was above me.

'You still here?' he slurred, and then turned into the kitchen. His words stung my newly found focus, like a bee sting on a perfect day at the beach.

'Do you want me to make you something to eat?' I asked, as if he was behaving perfectly reasonably.

He just mumbled and made to open a cupboard door, but gave up on the first attempt. He stumbled into the sitting room and body-slammed onto the couch, closing his eyes on contact. I got a blanket from the armchair and put it on him gently. I kissed his cheek, then I sat down on the chair and stared at him in the half-morning light, which was beginning to twinge orange. I stared out of the net curtains. I tried to remember the rhyme about the orange light, or was it about red? Did it count here in the big city, the red sky at night shepherd's delight, red sky in the morning shepherd's warning? Maybe I was being warned, first-hand, about the difficulties I would face trying to free Jules. I thought of his music and the nights in my student flat, when I had watched him sleep as I was doing now. I felt calm again.

When Sandra came downstairs, she walked by us and put on the TV. Then she brought the ironing board in. The protests were still on the news. The cameras zoomed in on the trees, where dreadlocked men and women were making tree houses. The police stood below, watching. I looked for Jules' face or his familiar dreads but didn't spot him. I didn't want to look too closely, as I was afraid of alerting Sandra to where he had been. She seemed to think he had been at a concert. My calmness was dissipating again as I watched her out of the corner of my eye. I imagined her as one of the she-devils who were pictured in the book. She'd probably suit being a Tibetan three-headed fury who ate your body as you died, so you could be reborn into the next life on land. She'd chew me up and spit me out, choking, sending me backwards into this human realm, where the world span backwards and not forward. Where the wheel was tread backwards, by the devolution from pure plankton and tapeworms into greedy, selfish, polluting, vain humans. Protesting and disabling machinery was not creating, and so what was the point? Animals and birds did nothing but create beautiful homes and endless offspring, all as perfect and innocent as themselves. When they killed each other, they did so for a reason. They didn't count how many Weight Watchers points were in the tomato sauce, full of dye and sugar, that they loaded onto the charred flesh of dead animals that they hadn't even killed themselves. Animals just were, and I wished I could just be too, but I knew that if I worked on Jules, and even Sandra, I could be taken from this realm of hell. Then I knew I could return to the sea of pure being and take Jules with me, even if we had to go through the mouth of Sandra. Our reverse journey would heal the wound that lay in my ribs and would take the knife out that Jules had put in my chest. The knife that fitted so exactly. Trying to cling onto my train of thought, I turned and trod up the carpeted cream stairs and returned to the underwater sea of my dreams.

27

When I woke up, all of that morning's clear vision was gone.

I had dreamt about my parents, that they were in a car underwater and were trying to get out. I waved at them, but they kept hitting on the doors. They screamed, and bubbles of air came up from their distorted faces as the car filled up with water like a cartoon. For the first time since they died I felt sad, and wondered would my life have been different if they had lived. I figured it would have been much simpler and that, at the very least, I would have never moved in here under their guidance. Perhaps I would be like my sisters, and I'd be doing a steady line with a local farmer and going to mass on Sundays. I tried to concentrate on non-violent resistance, the alternative to monkey wrenching. I called back the calmness and the clarity to quell the panic that was bubbling up from my lungs and shaking my skin.

It occurred to me that maybe the only solution was to join the Hare Krishnas. To shave my head and chant and sign over all my money. But I wasn't sure if orange was my colour.

I avoided the darkened sitting-room and met with Sandra in the bright clean kitchen, which stank of disinfectant and the toast that she was eating. She had returned to her usual self and barely deigned to greet me over her paper, with the headline, 'Father of five who hasn't worked a day in his life'. The headline was coupled with a picture of a young man surrounded by his young smiling children. I ate my cornflakes. Sandra left first, muttering. I followed her out the door to a phone box to ring work, feigning sickness. My manager replied with indifference.

I went looking for the library in Croydon. It was awkward to get to as it was in an unfamiliar area, surrounded by industrial high-rise office towers. I wandered against the commuter crowd, towards the South End, where I asked directions. I found the section on Babies and Pregnancy, pointed out by the thin, calm woman behind the desk. She pointed to a leaflet stand too, so I took a few on my way, and then dejectedly took down some large books and sat at a desk. I needed something to follow, something to guide me. They were filled with pictures of the embryo, day by day, from the beginning, which was now I supposed. The human embryo, it explained, shown lit by bright light, was indistinguishable from other life on sea or land. At this stage it looked like a fern, curled up like a seahorse. I smiled; this was it, this was what would save Jules, and me too. Maybe this was why I was there, why I had left Jamie, why Hippocampus had urged me forward, why I hadn't walked into a pond with rocks in my pocket. Maybe everything would be OK if I had the baby and Jules, I thought then, would be opened up to love and calm, and that was why I was there. We could create a symphony. We could adopt Jamie and bring him here. Jamie would even get better treatment on the NHS and would come back to me.

On the way out, I stopped in the small park in front, dwarfed by another office block but brightened by an erratic fountain. The smell of petrol and the sound of the traffic overwhelmed me. The skyscrapers on Wellesley Road shimmered like mirages in a desert. I couldn't face going back to the house, so I got the train into London from East Croydon station. I got the tube from London Bridge to the National Gallery, searching for more guidance in the paintings.

I wandered around the gallery in a daze, then went out to feed the pigeons in Trafalgar Square. Between the billboards there was the beautiful architectural grandeur and excitement of London. I was in the very heart of it; I felt that country girl's grip of fear and excitement again, mixed up in a swollen mash of envy for those who really belonged here. I decided that we had to move away from the soulless suburban heart of blandness that was Croydon, if I was to save Jules and the baby from Middle England evil.

I went over and picked up a few free magazines and sat down on the side of Nelson's Column, looking through them. A homeless man approached, trying to engage me in conversation, but I tuned him out, looking at flats to rent and rooms to share. I supposed I could have moved back onto campus but I figured we needed somewhere with energy and a new start.

I didn't want to share with 'Bubbly Kiwis' or party animals in Shepherd's Bush. So I returned the magazine to its metal box and walked back through the aimless tourists to the train station. When I got to the platform, I wrote down a number for an accommodation agency from an ad above the tracks. I had picked up an Evening Standard that seemed more promising. On the train I circled some interesting places, and braced myself to tell Jules the news in a calm and enlightened way. I even thought about my imminent exams, and resolved to make out a study timetable the next day so that I would be in a position to pass them.

They were eating pie and mash in front of the TV when I came in. I wasn't offered any, so I sat in the kitchen until they were finished.

'Hey, do you want to go to the local for a drink?' I said from the door.

'If you're buying,' Jules said, not looking away from the TV.

'But what about pudding Jules?' said Sandra, turning her head to glare at me.

I suppose she thought I was going to tell him about the whole doctor business, but she needn't have worried. I hummed a half-remembered mantra from the book in my head to tune out any doubts on the way there. I wanted to tell him what I knew, but first got his pint of cider and my half with blackcurrant. We sat down at a polished mahogany table in the clean but smoky newness of the O'Neill's pub that was the local. I had never been inside before. Sandra, who cursed the Irish for their very existence, was seemingly not averse to bad pints of Guinness and paying £1 for a packet of Tayto crisps. It was still like other English pubs, with wide, empty spaces between the bar and the tables. Also, there was the lack of noise. People sat and stared at the bar and the shelves of strange beers.

'I'm moving out,' I said, placing his cider on the table, 'Come with me.'

He grunted.

'We could move up to North London, you'd be nearer your friends.'

He didn't answer. I took this as a good sign, and continued.

'My grant would cover the rent, I'm sure.'

He still didn't answer.

'I'm pregnant,' I said, although I wasn't sure, but I needed a response.

His mouth opened, then he finally spoke.

'Oh right,' he said, 'I suppose we'd better move out then, Mum won't be happy.'

Then he got up and went to the fruit machine. I smiled and sipped the cider.

O'Hara asks me why I didn't tell the doctor, why I didn't go to the hospital, why I didn't have an abortion, why I didn't go home, why Jules never noticed or questioned why I did none of those things. I wonder why he doesn't ask Jules. I do not answer him. I cannot answer him. He says I have attachment issues, he says I have trust issues; he says I must have been sexually abused as a child. He asks me to remember.

'I am drowning,' I say, 'Drowning in this air.'

He frowns. When the nurse comes to collect me, he tells her to turn off the air conditioning in my room.

28

We moved into a one-bedroom flat above a launderette in Islington. It was the best I could get without a previous landlord's reference. The stylish loft apartments didn't want to know about an Irish student and her scruffy boyfriend. Though the price wasn't much less. I lied to Jules about the rent, which was to be handed weekly in cash to the launderette below.

Maud was a woman of indeterminate age and size. She had showed me the flat herself, though she could barely negotiate the two flights of stairs to the door of the flat, let alone the one up to the bedroom. The first flight was accessed by a burgundy door to the side of the launderette itself, which took us up to the storeroom door.

'Though you need to stay out of our way when we are coming up and down, mind,' she said the day she showed me up.

I nodded from behind.

She used her huge set of keys to open the door beside it, which went directly to another flight of stairs, carpeted in threadbare yellow and brown roses. They led to the sitting room. It was narrow and had thick, heavy net curtains, making the brown décor even duller. There was a brown velveteen couch with a matching armchair. It faced an old brown-veneer television. All grouped around a huge electric fire, which was set in a cream-tiled mantelpiece.

'Kitchen's over here,' she said as she moved towards a set of huge brown-veneer cupboards. She pulled them outwards to reveal a sink on one side and a two-ringed cooker with grill on the other. Pots and pans hung down on hooks above it. The fridge was between the door we came in and the cupboards.

'Now you run up them stairs and have a look at the bedroom and bathroom.'

I found a tiny bathroom with a blue toilet and a shower. The shower curtain was white, and mouldy at the bottom. The bedroom was tiny too, but there was a small double bed beneath the brown headboard. Smiling, I reached down and stroked the yellow roses on the nylon bedspread, imagining us lying there, undisturbed by Sandra. I ran back downstairs. Maud was still trying to catch her breath.

'I'll take it,' I said.

She looked at me suspiciously. 'Two months' rent down as a deposit and I'll want paying weekly in cash.'

I nodded and smiled again.

'And no funny business,' she added. 'Is it just you on your own love?'

'No I have a boyfriend. He's English,' I added for posterity.

She nodded her head again and headed for the door. I followed her step by step down the stairs, smiling and planning our escape. I know a piano would never fit up the stairs but I cast the thought aside.

Sandra gave me the evil eye for the next week or two and muttered a lot, but conceded her defeat. I am not sure if Jules told her about the baby then or after; either way, she never said anything to me. Maybe this was how mothers were supposed to be.

We left one Saturday in Mark's Bedford van. Jules was standing at the mouth of the chariot to freedom and, as I lugged the cardboard boxes into the van, it was like being freed from quicksand, a quagmire.

I never went out to Croydon again.

Jules didn't say much about the flat. I did all the unpacking when he headed off again with Mark. I managed to ditch the box that I found the tattoo magazines in, as I knew he wouldn't ask me about them. I planned to save him in this flat above a launderette, but I hadn't noticed the smell of washing powder on the day I viewed it. Too eager, I supposed, but some of the other flats I had seen hadn't even had their own toilet. And it was across from the Angel tube station. I saw this as another sign; I was the angel, Jules' guardian angel. I loved him, and I blamed Sandra for the way he was. I knew that he would flourish here, undisturbed by her. I stacked up my new books around the flat, mostly about yoga and reincarnation, books that I had told him I had found in the charity shop. Along with the other bargains, towels, sheets and throws. All much cheaper than I could afford, but still with the price tags removed. I stuck up a poster I had bought at The Natural History museum of a large fossil curling in on itself. Then I took it back down, crumpled it a bit and tore off a corner, to make it look like I had just taken it off a wall.

I did my repeat exams, my mind a bit sharper than before. The practicals went better this time, but I still went to the office and enquired about taking a year off. The bored secretary just handed me a ream of forms. A piano wasn't going to find its way up those stairs and, what with the baby coming, I had a sneaking suspicion I'd never go back. To throw Jules off the money scent, I got a job in a Jewish bakery a few tube stops away.

It was not the only branch of Rinkoff's, though it did not look like a franchise or a chain. It was old and dark, with black and white tiles on the floor and leaden windows with an orange film over them so that the displayed stock could be taken home at the end of the day by the staff, who all wore white caps, not the disposable kind. The caps were sent to the laundry and we wore a fresh one every day with a hairnet underneath. My hair always escaped at the edges. Magda, the old Eastern European lady who supervised me, would fuss and try to tuck it in.

The shop hadn't been done up since it opened; the older, more traditional customers didn't care, and the newer, trendier Islington types loved it for its originality and real ingredients, which we didn't advertise, but which they knew that we used. These young couples were disappointed when I spoke as I was Irish not Jewish, though they often assumed I was both. 'I never met an Irish Jewish person before,' they'd say; I'd smile and try to look busy so they wouldn't question me further. I wasn't sure if there were any Irish Jewish people either.

I started going to pregnancy yoga on Tuesday nights, on the way home. It was in the better part of Islington, in a tall, converted, brown brick house. I tried to reach for a calmness that I could inject into the tension of the flat. The class was filled with middle-aged women who all seemed to have wonderfully rich, absent husbands. Some of them had just had a baby and were already pregnant again. They talked about home births, pelvic floor exercises and birthing pools. When they came around to me I just smiled. They didn't pursue it, and eventually stopped asking me to coffee mornings.

I just went home, where I walked on eggshells. Our magical flight from Sandra had not improved Jules for the better. I took on her role for the first week as best I could, but with improvements. I made healthy TVP-based vegetarian meals from scratch and dropped our laundry below for a service wash once a week. It came back already ironed. I made him tea every morning before work and left it on the brown bedside locker. He never thanked me. His moodiness increased, if anything. He blamed the noise and the pollution and the people and me, of course. He accused me of all sorts, quizzing my whereabouts every day if he was sober enough. The box for recycling filled up with empty Scrumpy Jack cider cans, rolled cigarette butts inside. Their smell eclipsed by the laundry. He was supposedly writing music at home. When I'd enquire about how it was going he'd get angry. The violin case lay unopened for days, unless his friends had been. They came during the day, mostly when I was not there. I came home to empty cupboards and used towels. I started buying ready meals. They didn't eat them, at least.

Within a week of us finally being able to share a bed, he started falling asleep on the couch. I stayed to my side of the bed, hoping that he would come up in the night. My metronome sat on the bedside locker. When I couldn't sleep, I opened its wooden cover and set it to ticking, moving my fingers, practising under the covers as it ticked away the useless, slow seconds. The grey light and the noise from the street brought him upstairs just as I was getting up.

I had arranged the bathroom shelves with new toiletries and bought a stainless-steel rack that held up with plastic suckers. He had stopped shaving and had started growing a patchy beard. It had strange orange patches. I'd stroke it in the mornings when I didn't have to go in and made jokes about his Irish heritage. He'd scowl and turn over.

On Sundays, we'd get up late and go to the local café. Beans, chips, strong tea and The Observer. Then I'd turn for the flat when we got to the tube station. He would visit Sandra, to eat his dinner of vegetables and gravy and watch mindless television. I could envision the whole afternoon: her giving out about me and pursing her lips up during the ad breaks, the talk about terrorism and of the very work- shirkers that her son had become. He'd arrive back every Sunday night, slightly sloshed but tenser than usual, and find fault with something, then talk about getting a better television for a while.

So I had Sundays to myself. I tried to practise the yoga moves from class in the tiny sitting-room. I'd go swimming in the public pool, though preferred the quietness of the weekday mornings. On these Sundays, unlike my other days off, splashing children disturbed my lengths.

Jules never asked me what I did when he wasn't there on Sundays. Perhaps Sandra had convinced him that the Irish don't sin on Sundays. Though I would have thought that all day Sunday was a better day to meet an imaginary lover, rather than during the week at work, wearing a white cap and covered in sticky pastry mix.

My stomach rounded and got bigger; I was not sure if it was the baby or the day-old bakery items I brought home. I sometimes felt fluttering, like fish fins brushing against my insides. But I did not go to the doctor, and Jules didn't ask. The old women at work must have assumed that I did.

I hardly noticed as Jules got drunker and meaner and my soul throbbed with a dull ache, as if it had closed over and got used to it. As I was no longer at college Mona had no way of keeping in contact. Of course I meant to ring her, and had even gone to a phone box to call her, but had put the receiver down again. I mean, what would I have said? That I was now living in a grotty flat in London that I could afford to buy twice over? That I was pregnant, but hadn't been to the doctor? That I was working in a Jewish bakery, selling cakes to old ladies, wearing a white hat and a white coat, although I didn't need the money? That I was living with the rude, anti-social boyfriend I had brought to her home the last time I saw her, over a year ago? That we weren't having sex because he fell asleep on the couch, and when he woke in the night he pissed in an empty cider can so he didn't have to come upstairs at all? That he was supposed to be working on the music that he now had a degree in? That he never missed a trip to his mother's on a Sunday, and when he came home he spoke to me even less than usual. That on Sundays he didn't accuse me of having an affair, as he did most other days. That this twenty year old girl, who had won a thousand cheap gold trophies on marble stands for piano playing, had dropped out of college because she'd come to the conclusion that she'd been sent down to this hellhole of a life to suffer, so that she could save this awful boy from a fate worse than hell or limbo, and that she didn't go to church, and that she had worshipped heathen gods, and yes, she knew she could come home, because she was not even married to him like you were to George C, but she had made her bed so she'd lie in it, until she reached a state of enlightenment through her good deeds and her care not to kill either directly or indirectly another living thing on this ugly earth. That she felt

134

smaller than one of the ants that roamed through the kitchen cupboards.

I couldn't tell her or anyone else all this because they wouldn't believe that that was the way it was, but I thought that someday it would all work out because I believed that the baby could save Jules.

I never said too much about the baby in case he told me to have an abortion, or Sandra carried out her threat. I was doing everything I needed to find forgiveness, being celibate like a nun as my growing stomach had turned Jules from me. I knew that someday he would see this, and he gave me glimmers of hope from time to time by hugging me and telling me that I was all he had. Sometimes he cried in front of me, in the days before his next giro was due.

O'Hara asks me about religion; I tell him I am a Catholic, I worship the cult of the Virgin Mary, I tell him I am a Buddhist, I am a pagan, I tell him God is water.

I tell him nothing.

29

I talked to the baby and it listened, swimming in my depths. I imagined it like the seahorse in the book, but that it had maintained the shape. Somehow, I told it, I would help it swim through the streets after its release, through the dirt and traffic of the North London streets, to navigate the concreted-over rivers that I knew must flow beneath our feet.

On Sundays, I wished I could go into Rinkoff's and rid myself of the awful feelings of hollowness, guilt and inertia that I had on days off.

Jules still didn't know about all the money I had, because somehow I had never told him. I had always found it embarrassing. It seemed strange that I could go anywhere and do anything and not have to worry about it. I didn't want it to be like that. Mona had always warned me not to be used for my money. If you don't tell someone something straight away it gets harder and harder to do so, and Jules barely trusted me as it was. Telling him after all that time would have called everything I said into question. I could see the rows that would follow, screaming through the canals of my brain. I had had such a belly-full of Jules and Sandra telling me how hard it was when 'Dad' passed away. I imagined the interest piling up; the statements still came to Mona's.

I did all the food shopping and paid the bills. That used up the money from the bakery. Jules spent the proceeds of his giro in the off-licence and on the magazines that he hid under the sofa. I had found them when I was hoovering. I longed for the magazines that I had got rid of when we moved in. They seemed less seedy than the new ones, which now joined the tattooed girls in my head. They popped up at inappropriate moments in the shop, when people unconsciously struck a familiar pose while bent to arrange their shopping, or leant over to point at a particular cake.

The day I left was a Thursday. I had a day off from Rinkoff's. Jules hadn't made it up the stairs at all so far that week. When I came downstairs the room stank of laundry detergent and stale alcohol, with a whiff of urine. I pulled the curtains and opened up the sash window. The traffic roared outside. Jules jerked in his sleep, then opened and closed his drying lips. He half-opened his eyes, then opened them fully and shot up when he saw me staring at him from inside the window. How strange my silhouette must have looked in his half-drunken state. When he moaned and lay back down, I walked towards the kitchenette and switched on the kettle. Then I heard him leave the couch for the toilet. When he came back downstairs he leaned on the alcove's entrance. I ignored him, though I could feel his bleary, bloodshot eyes on me; I just stared at the kettle, waiting for it to boil, and then opened the cupboard, leaning back to plonk the charity shop china mugs down and throw the teabags into them. I turned and pushed past him, crouching down for the fridge. He stared as if he could hear my thoughts. I fumbled for the milk.

'Not working today?' he said in an accusatory fashion.

I didn't answer.

He reached forward and viciously pinched my hip. I gasped and dropped the milk.

He kept talking, ensured now that he had my attention.

'I missed signing on yesterday so I have to go down there, fucking hate that place, it's ridiculous, I'm going to apply for an Arts Council grant, I must call to the college and get the forms.'

He had been signing on from the squat in Holland Park, so it involved a long trip and a longer wait. He went to get his cheque every two weeks, going straight from the couch at dawn in case the proceeds of the giro got redistributed at the squat. He usually gave me twenty pounds out of it, but always ended up borrowing it back. When I asked him to get shopping, he bought Kwik Save brand food that I couldn't eat. So I had stopped asking.

The moaning about the Arts Council was growing more frequent. He'd rant and rave about the lack of support for musicians and the Art Council's collusion with the government, who must have him on a protesters' database or something. I had gone over the various points, like having to have work to show, but this just set him off into an unrelenting sulk, followed by the usual drunkenness, which was now my fault due to me not having believed in his music.

He never talked like this when his friends came, as they did even more often now. The water was off again at the squat. They talked about the bypass, the protest there and the tunnels. I'd sit and listen on my day off, and my non-participation was taken for lack of understanding.

Jules' violin became a fiddle when they were around. Folk songs to be played at protests were discussed. My pregnancy was celebrated by them, though, and this often got Jules around to talking about how we would bring the baby up. Simply, breastfed, and with only oranges and saucepans to play with. A girl called Figs, who could sing 'Dirty Old Town' to Jules' accompaniment, had started calling more often than the rest. I knew when she had been there as my moisturiser had been used. He answered her questions about his dad, how he died. He said that corporations had killed him, his was cancer caused by chemicals, the chemicals he had worked with, the chemicals that they profited too much from to ban. I suspected he was sleeping with her, but I didn't want to sound like him.

She rarely spoke to me, only telling me off once for eating a Kit Kat.

'We're boycotting Nestle,' she said scornfully. 'The breast milk thing, you should know.'

I ate it later.

He never talked to me about the baby, the simple life we would lead in a bender, or the evils of vaccinations, when we were alone.

He just moaned about grants. I wasn't in the mood to take it today, so I just kept making the tea and said nothing as I wiped up the spilt milk with some budget kitchen roll. It was the white kitchen roll that refocused my mind as I watched it absorb the milk in a solemn, slow-moving circle on the tiles. I took the tea, handed one to Jules, and took mine to the bedroom so I could think. But he followed me. I sat on the bed, looking down, drinking the tea, trying to drown out his rantings from the door jamb. I looked at the carpet, nylon with yellow roses, and felt ill. Jules finished up and said he was off to the off-licence again and slammed the door, indicating his bad mood, which I didn't care about anymore.

I toed the yellow roses, still looking down, then lay back on the bed and stared at the ceiling. The damp patches whorled around me, as close to my underwater palace as I could be. My hip throbbed.

I supposed that, with my job reference, I could now get a nice yuppie loft up the road a bit. I could just rent it and leave right now, but my guilt doubled about Jules. I knew he'd be forced back to his mother's and that he'd be doomed. I did love him, and according to Sandra there was nothing worse than a child who had no father. Would our child be cruel like him if I left? I needed someone to talk to, and suddenly I missed Jamie so much I thought I'd throw up. The dry, chemical smell of the launderette overwhelmed me. I wanted to ring home so badly that I had to squeeze my nails into my palms and promise myself that I would soon. Soon, after I moved. Then maybe Jules could stay here and get housing benefit or something and we could try to go back to the beginning, go on dates and rekindle the romance, and he could go for counselling. My mind seemed different, like the pinch he had given me had focused my skull, or my fontanelles had opened and air had come in and I could imagine a sky above that narrow gap that I saw every day, above the city traffic.

I decided to do some yoga, but the sitting room was too messy.

He came back in as I was hoovering; I had opened all the windows. He walked to the fridge-freezer and opened it and took out some awful frozen thing; he was opening the microwave when I turned off the hoover.

'Let's go out to lunch, get a Chinese or something,' I said, dreading a bad reaction. 'There's a good one across from work.'

He shrugged his approval, turned and put on his leather jacket, which he had slung on the couch, and nodded his head towards the door. I grabbed a poncho and followed. We stood outside the entrance to the flat as if confined by the idea, and then he turned left towards the tube and I followed. We went down into the dry wind of the escalators, not talking, visibly far apart. I imagined us as a famous couple who the paparazzi had photographed, to be put in a gossipy magazine. They would have analyzed the scene, with arrows indicating our true feelings, as illustrated by our body language. My sisters would have flicked through it in the hairdressers.

They seemed to know him in the restaurant. It took me aback; I suppose I had never imagined that anyone else, except me and the Holland Park crew, recorded his existence these days, well, apart from the dole office and his mother. We went up and down to the copper pans of the buffet and got our food. I ate ravenously, as if I'd never eaten before. Jules picked at the food, complaining that it was too cold.

I imagined what it would have been like, life for us in a remote province in China, as I ate the food. I saw us in an arranged marriage in the heat, where I cooked elaborate spicy meals while he went out to work in the rice fields. We had watched a documentary about this once. Jules had said it was the way things were before corporations had wrecked the earth. I saw him come home, tanned and dressed in dusty, loose cotton trousers, kissing me as he entered our simple hut. I would lay out a beautiful meal for us and the child at the low table while Jules and I exchanged proud glances. We'd eat, then put the child to bed, and we'd make love in front of the wood stove. Jules would fall asleep in my arms, and then get up early to go back to work.

I saw this stereotypical, romantic dream of a simple life, and thought about how the same couple I imagined probably dreamed of a life in London, of eating in restaurants, of having money in the bank, of being able to compose music on benefits without judgment, of central heating and carpets and soft beds, and paid employment that didn't render them crippled. Still, I despaired to myself of the life I was leading, going nowhere with Jules, his apathy and procrastination and his coldness. I refocused on him: chewing slowly, with a lack of enthusiasm. I confronted him,

'Have you been here before?'

'Yes,' he said.

'Why?'

'To keep an eye on you, why else?'

He seemed to take my silence as some kind of acceptance, and started shovelling the food down faster. The waiter came to check on us, but seemed to accept my weak smile. He nodded and silently removed himself from the table. Another waiter walked by with a line of seahorses on a skewer for the next table. The claustrophobia of our relationship closed in on me. I imagined how I must have looked through the shop window. I put down my cutlery slowly and walked to the cash register, paid and left. I went towards work; Jules wasn't following me; I was relieved, so I picked up the pace and arrived there in the time it took me to stop chewing. They were surprised to see me on my day off, and as dumbfounded as I was when I told Magda that I was giving my week's notice. She smiled sadly but began writing a 'help wanted' sign even as I stood there, petrified about what I'd just done. That was the thing about London, you were expendable, another Irish girl in the crowd. Perhaps they were relieved I wouldn't be asking for maternity leave. I breathed in the apricot jam as I left, surrounding myself in its sticky comfort for the last time.

When I came out again Jules was standing there, glowering; I turned left and walked away. He followed, still glowering; I could feel him behind me, even on this busy street. His presence was all-consuming but not like Jamie's had been, before the medication. His was looming, he was devouring me, not completing me, not enveloping me in softness.

He caught up. 'What were you doing, embarrassing me like that?'

I didn't answer and kept walking. He grabbed my shoulder and I shrugged him off as he tried to turn me around to face him; I kept walking. He shouted after me.

'I'm going back to my mother's. That baby probably isn't even mine. I'm going to live with the others in Newbury. I'm going with Figs. At least she stands up for herself. Bitch.'

I would have usually given in at that point, but I was closed now to what he did or said. I saw a park so I walked in and sat down, shivering. He didn't follow. We'd had more interaction in the past few hours than we'd had in months. I stared at a bird in a tree and longed for its freedom, longed to fly away. There I was, pregnant, no job, no boyfriend, no reason to get up, not even an addiction to blame for it, and it was all going around in my head, like the Waltzer at the fairground. Jules was the boy treading the boards in my mind, collecting the money as it spun.

I knew I couldn't face the crush of the tube, so I waited for a bus. The first one that came was going to Oxford Street. I surprised myself by staying on till the end. I got out, and on impulse I went to the bank and took out a huge sum of money. I held it in my fist and took it to Selfridges where, in a frenzy, I bought a rug and curtains and throws and new towels, as if to cover up the grime of my chosen life of destitution that was all a fake. To wash away all the frugality and environmentalism, which was just a finger in the dyke of the rising sea.

Water was in all these things. Water whispered in the ears of the men who ordered these things be made and sold. Water would use them all, to rise up and return, and would not be stopped by fair trade cotton or monkey wrenches.

I tried on some clothes, things I would never wear, with flowing fabrics and bright colours that revealed how much money I had, but I didn't buy anything else. All the time I had spent hiding my wealth couldn't be undone in a day. I had changed enough already. I began to feel panicky and out of control. My panic took over, and I felt vomit rising into my mouth in the changing room. I hastily pulled a plastic bag up, emptied it and puked, but it was only a little undigested spicy soup. I had puked on a new purple towel. Here I was, in an airless, windowless room, lightless building, in a crammed and filthy city without a sky. I was buying things I didn't need to fill the hole that gaped wider than the hidden sky and threatened to suck the city and all its contents in.

Then I knew what I needed to do; I needed to see the sea.

The only place I knew that had a sea here was Brighton. I went to the nearest tube station and went to Victoria. I walked in feeling calmer, and grabbed my bags around me like modern armour against the drunks who filled the station. The station roof mimicking the sky cruelly, its height even letting birds in. The destinations clacked into view, endlessly flipping as I walked to the end platforms that went to Brighton. I was still flanked by shops and buying and consuming, right to the end of where it was possible to fall off the edge, onto the rails. Where the mice ran around the idling Brighton Express.

I had bought a first-class ticket at the machine, determined to let go of my self-imposed poverty. It struck me that I was an orphan running away to see the seaside. I laughed. I kept laughing, and then I tried to calm down as we trundled past East Croydon station, out of the city, the housing growing less dense and the blocks of soulless flats getting progressively lower as the sky got wider.

I ordered tea in a fancy paper cup and half-burned my mouth; it tasted of nothing, despite its price. I caught amused glances from the businessmen whose eyes twinkled from behind their newspapers occasionally, clearly not used to such a specimen in first-class. I was sure they expected that when the ticket inspector came he would grab me by the scruff of the neck and drag me into the baggage hold, where I belonged.

I wished for a newspaper that I could hide behind, but resorted to reading the back of other people's. One man gently folded his and handed it to me; I tried to protest but he stopped me with a gesture, and so I read the nearly-not-as-interesting-close-up news for the last leg of the journey into Brighton. I thought I would see the sea from the train, but had to ask for directions when I got into the hangar of Brighton Station.

I wandered out of the station in a daze, not really having understood the instructions, wanting to ask again, but I kept going in the distinctly different air that flooded my brain and began to loosen it. I found the seafront, or it found me, my feet pulled by its magnetism. It was very different to the sea of my childhood, the Atlantic Ocean. Though I supposed they were all the same, ultimately.

This sea seemed different, though; I couldn't remember what sea this was; there was no land in sight. It was endless and flat. The beach was brown and pebbled, and the pier loomed over it all like a spindly spider. The sea here was so contained, but I breathed it in then crunched along the beach, forgetting for a while the imminent choices that had to be made. The smell of chips wafted towards me, and I ate some paddling along in the freezing water. They were doused in vinegar and salt and I ate them with a wooden spear. I remembered all the times that my sisters had asked for take-away chips, and how my mother would say that they should watch their faces and skin.

I compared the gentle swashing of the waves to one of those sea noise tapes that I had bought to relax me, but that just reminded me of being in the flat. I knew that I never wanted to see the flat again. I supposed that Jules wouldn't report me missing or anything. It scared me, though, I loved Jules, and despite everything he was my only friend; I wanted to cry with rage and frustration for all the wasted time. I kept walking, with the bags of towels from Selfridges that I had bought what seemed like eons ago. The towels and the throws all useless now to my plans. Only the towels might come in handy to dry my wet feet, which had now turned purple in the autumn water. I shivered as I dried them.

I needed to go indoors. I handed in my bags at the reception of the Sea Life Centre, which accommodated the tourist office. I figured I should get a map and find somewhere to stay, and I picked up a few brochures and flicked through them while wandering about the exhibition. I wandered to the Irish section last, and came to a stop by the seahorses. I stared at them, the male above the female, apologetic for the fact that he could not save them from this fate worse than death, trapped in a glass tank in the bright lights in this exhibition hell. She stayed below secretly, not wanting to live anymore. I pressed my face against the glass. Someone asked me eventually if I was alright, and when I shook my head they brought me to the manager's office. It was all white, and I closed my eyes and began crying all over again at the awfulness of this place without real light. I decided to go back to Ireland.

There is a piano in the common room. O'Hara encourages me to try it, as does the Occupational Therapist, Vivian. I cannot. I cannot lose myself now, or I might miss the signs. Jamie and Melody are sending me signs. Sometimes they are in the patterns in the paint peeling underneath the windowsill, sometimes in the rain rivulets on the windowpane.

I look out into the garden; there are sunflowers planted by the other residents. Their heads tilt up and their leaves rise in a sun salute, beseeching, pleading to be made human. They do not know what it is really like, how we suffer, how long our lives are, what we have sacrificed, the tortuous thoughts that haunt us throughout the night. We cannot even worship the sun, for now it is killing us, blackening us, burning us, to punish us, as we are ungrateful. We slather ourselves in oil to protect ourselves, oil tells us to, but the rays get through. Sunflowers can boldly turn their faces to the sky, brazenly follow the sun as it wheels across the sky.

I imagine this; sun hot, full face, arms upstretched, growing closer and closer to worship, sleeping only to want for its return, glory in the rain, sliding within, water loving me, filling me, helping me reach higher and higher, till the day the sun fades and loses interest in me and I fade and melt, pecked by birds, oozing my oil into their blood, flying up, soaring closer and raining down, back to the earth to rest inside for winter, curled up, until my lover the sun returns and I rise again, multiplied, every surface multiplied. I will cover the earth someday; my lover promised me this as his heat licked me. When they are gone, my love, he says, we will dominate the earth, then the sea will abate.

In his office, O'Hara asks me about grief. He asks why I do not feel it now, or did not feel it then. People write about death a lot in books. It seems to spark a creative impulse, a quickening, a camera shutter with a wide aperture that takes in the whole scene and everyone in it. It x-rays them so that their insides are laid out, end to end, around the walls of the room, like The Bayeux Tapestry. How everyone felt then and into the future, the irreparable nature of it, and all of the blame. Who killed my parents, whose fault was it, who did it, who had to live with it for the rest of their life, whose family was forever darkened by their presence? I see them in their front room, staring at the fire, afraid to enter the pub in case it goes silent, afraid to go out to the shop, afraid to see me or my sisters or George C, our only protector, afraid to look at me, did they look at me at the funeral? Were they even there? Did they see that I wasn't bothered? Did that bother them more? As though they saw the innocence that would be shattered when the grief hit me, but the grief never has, not even now, not even now. I imagine Mona knows that now, she knows that all the years she waited for the grief to catch up with me were in vain.

What I was feeling was what I had always felt, the greyness, the post-nuclear greyness of this poisoned world which I was glad Jamie had been taken from, had swum to. Had swum from. I was now that person, I had killed them as well as my parents. Mona had taken a monster into her cave, a monster cuckoo who had swallowed up her son, biding her time to do so, so both were swallowed, both were taken and couldn't ever be replaced.

O'Hara asks me if I hold myself responsible for the death of my parents as well. He says I need to accept that their death was an accident. That a local man was charged with drunken driving in connection with their death. Everyone knew who this man was except me. I tell him that no one had ever told me who he was, no one had ever said it at school, even though his daughter was in the class above me and she had watched me from the side of the playground. The daughter of the man who was waiting to redeem himself.

I don't blame that man, though O'Hara suggests I do. I blame the oil. I tell him this. He ignores me. I cannot be silent. I cannot play the game anymore. I tell him.

'Oil says be quiet, stop thinking, consume, consume to the beat, the beat of the fairground that sneaks on empty land and crushes the weeds before they grow too big, beats you down as you spin and feel sick and consume, and sugar shoots through your brain, and you consume and consume to the beat of the drum, in the shops that echo, in the factories where other humans, human children who once were you, lose their hands and arms and choke on oil, and you don't care because you have your fashionable clothes and your chemical soap and your Pot Noodles. Everything is less and less real, more and more oil, water says give the earth to oil, oil says you control me, you think you control me as you call me out of the ground, do you hear me calling you? You brave the depth of the ocean to bring me unto the *land, you tear through lakes, you bump through sand, you love me, you cannot get enough of me, lay in me, cover yourselves in me, drown in me, I will kill you faster than water, water is cruel, it will pretend to keep you afloat. I will not, let me be your water, we cannot get along, it is me or him. I can walk on water. I am Exxon Valdez, I will pour down on the earth, destroy them all, stop you flying, walking, breathing. You tell me you are tired, stop fighting me, succumb, I am rich, scoop your hands in me. You watch from behind your headphones as you crumple another wrapper and throw it on the ground and the beat goes on, tells you not to trust others, to stay indoors, to watch TV. Hippocampus laughs and tells you yes, this is what we wanted, we need protection from the sun, the elements, they are trying to stop us, we won't be stopped, we want to be dry, dry like the opposite of how it was when we were surrounded by water and its depth and weight, we want to be airless and plastic and light and float, we will always float, we will mass together and float, we will live forever, so high we reach the sun, so it can finally melt us to a crisp and we can float back down, carbon again, weightless, nothing, return to all, return to one, slow motion, speed up, rewind to that point where we began and crushed together in the dark, we want to go back there please.'*

He calls the nurse. He tells her I cannot play the piano anymore. He says that I must be confined to my room.

Part 3

Long-term Potentiation

30

When I stepped off the plane at Dublin airport, I felt momentarily calmer.

I booked into a hotel in the city centre from a freephone in the arrivals lounge. Rachel was at the airport; she had been sent by Mona. I barely recognised her. She was nervous around me, her eyes darting left and right constantly, as if planning her escape route from this lunatic sister. She was pregnant too, about five months on. She showed me the scan before we even got back to the short-term car park. I did not have one to exchange, so I said nothing.

She lived in the Dublin suburb of Blackrock, but planned to return home too. She was seeking planning permission for the home of their dreams, beside what was now Fionnuala's. She did not suggest that I stay with her. I was relieved, as I feared the suburbs; they were probably the same in all cities, and I feared another Croydon of horror waiting. We agreed to meet for dinner soon but made no concrete arrangements. Rachel said that Fionnuala came to Dublin to shop regularly, and would ring me. We drove in her black Lexus through the unfamiliar streets. She asked me about college. I told her I was taking a year off. Then she stopped abruptly; she apologized that she couldn't get me any closer to the hotel with the one-way system, but pointed me in its direction.

Dublin seemed less comforting than even London, and it had none of the familiarity and routine of my home village. I imagined Jules and Sandra's energy dragging me back to them; their lock on me circled my dreams. I tried to make myself understand our relationship so that it could not happen again. I had stayed with a man who had hated me. I had been free to go the whole time and now I had, but it was too late to ever fully escape them now.

I rang Jamie. Mona was frosty when she answered, but she called him to the phone. He didn't say much and I eventually hung up. The hotel room was bare, but clean and modern. I started unpacking my things. The towels I had bought in Selfridges were useless here at the hotel. I stuffed them in the bin; I tried to throw away London and Jules with them, but they didn't fit. I turned away from them and read through the hotel directory, which kept me calm with its useless information.

I went to a doctor first thing the next day, the one named on the hotel's folder. I gave my address as the hotel; he sent me straight to the hospital when I told him I had had no medical attention so far. It was an old red brick hospital, a walk from the hotel.

I had to wait in the queue with all the other pregnant women. They asked me how far on I was. The conversation stopped abruptly when I said I didn't know. When I was eventually scanned, they said that through the cold jelly they could see that I was nearly seven months pregnant, and that everything looked fine. It was a girl, they told me. I saw her there, swimming in black and white. I took the print-out, mesmerised. The nurse told me to go back to the doctor the next day to book myself in for the delivery.

I extended my stay in the hotel; they offered me a discount, though I didn't ask. I paid in cash, withdrawn from the counter of the bank nearby. The bank staff advised me to get a cash card. I didn't have the energy to look for a flat or to go back to the doctor. I had no address to give him, just the hotel. The staff were nice, if polite. They said nothing about my condition. I rang Jamie every night. During the day, I walked the streets in the crisp weather. When it rained, I went to the museums and breathed in their human history. Trying to absorb it, trying to belong.

I even met Rachel again in Clerys; she seemed not to notice I was pregnant. She was anxious. The fact that I met her in the children's section of Clerys seemed not to alert her. I supposed she saw me as sexless and as unlikely to be pregnant. Her rural upbringing had closed her mind.

I decided I would bring the child up in cities; we would travel the world together, by ship where possible, and I would bring music to

152

the masses, inspired by the love and oneness I would feel when she was born.

I let my sister make her excuses and leave. I was lost in my imagination. I was with my daughter, her in a sling. Traversing cities in my mind, meeting new and open people with whom we would find mutual companionship; I could create music and beauty, and feel like I wasn't alone anymore.

Christmas was coming. Mona had thawed somewhat, and had invited me back for the holidays. I took the bus to Dún Laoghaire and stood on the pier, watching the ships go out and marvelling at the grey, churning mass that made the gigantic ferries fade into a pinprick in its magnitude. I knew I should tell Mona about the baby before I got back. I had decided to call her Melody. I rubbed my stomach as I talked to her. I told her about the sea. I imagined how her childhood would differ from mine. She would understand the same strange feelings of loss as Jamie and me, but I could guide her, talk her through all of that.

Mona collected me from the bus. Her face was hard but she hugged me, then she stepped back and looked at my stomach.

'Ah, Marina,' she said, 'You've got yourself in a mess.'

I didn't reply.

Before we got out of the car, she asked me not to tell Jamie. George was at the pub as usual. It was Christmas Eve. Jamie was waiting by the tree. He was taller now, taller than me. I hugged him so hard I thought I'd crush the baby.

The baby responded with a kick so intense that I thought I would fold up. I sat down on the sofa. Mona looked worried. I wondered was I going into labour. Though it was a bit early, it was not an impossibility. I talked to my belly constantly, muttering against the pain. It stopped.

Jamie sat beside me on the sofa. We watched 'It's a Wonderful Life', and it was as if I had never left. I leaned my head on his shoulder. He leaned his head over mine.

'Everything's going to be OK now Marina,' he said.

I couldn't reply; tears rolled down my face.

'Don't worry, she says she'll be here soon to see us,' he whispered.

I lifted my head to look at him.

'I can hear her.'

She kicked in response.

Mona had made up the spare room. The house was smaller than my parents', but still had four bedrooms. Before he went to bed, Jamie came and sat by my bed and watched me. Mona looked in and said goodnight, taking him to bed.

'We'll talk on Boxing Day,' she said, turning off my light.

I awoke again and again to pee; I lurched each time in the pain. Jamie heard me cry out. He was there when my waters broke. He called Mona.

Mona decided to try to get us to the hospital; I had not even unpacked my bag. Heaving with the waves of contractions, I made my way down the stairs. The tidal lurches gathered force in the car.

At the hospital, they hooked me up to the monitor that drew the waves on the screen. I could see the contractions coming as they rose up to engulf me. The monitor beeped incessantly. The baby did not want to come out. Mona stayed with me, though Jamie was left in the corridor. She looked worried. More doctors arrived. They were coming to take her out, even if she did not want to come.

She arrived by Caesarean. Though I was groggy, they put her in the box beside the bed. The Christmas baby, they called her. There was tinsel wrapped around the railings on the bed.

Mona and Jamie came in when they were all gone. Mona was unsure what to say, but at least she was there. I felt dead inside. She was born. I looked in sadness at her helplessness in the plastic box. I knew how she felt but I could not comfort her. Jamie was different; he was happy when he looked at her. It was as though we had swapped places.

I was back at the hospital where I had been born. Where my parents had died. Where Jamie had been born, and where I had felt

154

hope for the first time. And now there she was too, and I wasn't ready for her. I hadn't planned it like this. The Holland Park crew had talked about home births in benders. Glowing placentas and glowing mothers at one with their babies, nothing like this.

The day after Boxing Day, Mona took us home in silence; George smiled at her, and weakly at me.

Mona had bought a pram in the sales. George had brought Jamie's cot down from the attic and put it in my room. I asked him to move it to the other spare room.

I stayed on past the holidays. I fed her the bottles that I prepared blurry-eyed and she cried. Jamie returned from school each day with Mona and went straight to her side. He told her what I had told him. She listened. I thought about her conception from the coldness that was Jules. I tried to remember the exact moment. I could not; surely I should have known. I turned it over and over in my head, looking for a moment of tenderness where she could have seeped through, unaffected. There were none. I thought about his darkness, enveloping her from the inside. It was like an orange tree with black, rotten fruit, forcing its way up through her intestines.

Mona booked the christening for the second week in February.

The phone calls from Sandra began; Mona fielded them though she wanted me to take them, but I wouldn't, I couldn't. In a trance, I waited for them to come for us and take us back to the place that was worse.

'She has a right to be angry,' Mona said as she put down the phone.

I could hear the shouting even after the receiver was put down.

George had got satellite television installed. Sky News rolled endless doom across the bottom of the screen. Blizzards raged across America. The worst in history they said. A plane crashed in Africa, ploughing through Kinshasa, killing hundreds. Chechens fought gun battles with Russian soldiers. 820,000 gallons of oil gushed into the seas at Rhode Island. I was afraid.

155

I had tried not to be afraid, not to scorn. I had tried to fit in, I had tried the big city life, the college, the boyfriend, meditation, bending myself into shape with yoga, and all the things that they said I was supposed to do. Should I have told Melody to do the same, should I have told Jamie, should I have sent them out into the world and told them that it all made sense, when it didn't? Could I have bought more things for her? Buggies, nappies and baby food, plastic toys that would end up adrift on the ocean, choking creatures that thought they were food?

I saw the footage of the tunnels at the Newbury bypass; the protesters were being dragged out of the trees in handcuffs. Arrested for trying to stop the diggers, armed only with shovels and Kryptonite bike locks. They could not stop the tide. I recognised some faces as they were led away in handcuffs.

Sandra rang again. Mona talked to her, and told me they were coming to see Melody. Mona went to the airport to collect them with George. On the television, a ferry in Sumatra sank, and one hundred people returned to the sea.

It was Jamie's idea, but it was what I wanted. We walked to the shore, ignoring the neighbours' stares. Mona had obviously not spread the good news. I was weak; my stomach hurt from pushing the pram. I gave it to him, he said it was the males who should carry the babies, and we walked together, not past him like I did before, but with him. I followed him. He walked ahead of me with her; she did not cry anymore. I knew she could swim there. The wind told the waves to be quiet, to let us go back, if that's what we wanted. We had to go back.

When I woke up I was here, but I knew by their faces that they had got there. That they lay curled up in the dark, waiting for me to join them.

O'Hara tells me it was the very same man who had killed my parents who pulled me out of the water. The other two got away before he could save them too.

The dust plays in the beam of light from the small window above the door.

I tell O'Hara everything I know.

'The oil rises up, bubbling out of the earth, reaching out to misguided men lost and wandering far from the sea, as it will not allow them to go back. It is liquid too; it tempts them. You can choose again, it says, it is not simply land or sea; you do not have to take one side or the other. Some creatures can live between the two, briefly checking out the other; only the birds and the flying fish can have all three. But oil will destroy them all. The oil whispers, lubricating the new thought channels like the insides of whelk shells, which it fills up too. I will make you master of all, it says to their ears, the whispers filter down, slide down to the centre. I can choke the birds, punish them, the fish and the trees, I can come alive in plastic, I will multiply and cover earth and sea, multiplying, seeping and crushing, across the earth, the sea, choking you all, the master of all. It tells them where to find it, more, under tar sands, under lakes, destroy it all, it says, and I will be the king of all. It calls the others oozing from fruits to join it, to destroy you. You eat it, you rub it on your face, it clogs your veins, it chokes your air, and you want more.

'Now, even the animals have started returning. You say they are becoming extinct, but I say they are walking back into the sea, the lake, the rivers. It started with the lemmings. They wanted to return to the primordial soup, to start again. They could stop us and our destruction of their homes if they wanted. The dogs could rip out our throats as we sleep. The rats could have our soft, vulnerable babies as they lie helpless in their cots. No, they lie down in the dirt, and decompose into the groundwater and go back to the sea.

'Guinea pigs captured from the wild kill their first litter, so that they do not have to live in captivity.

O'Hara says it all happened because of what age I was when my

157

parents died. The age of first sexual awakening, and that I thought God had punished me for this by taking my parents away. He says that's why I killed Jamie and Melody; he says they stood for sex and desire. Catholic Guilt made me kill them.

We are beneath again, I went back, I returned too, they are me, my children, our brothers and sisters, our mother, us, our neighbours, we, we are, I am. You fall down because you cannot. We are invincible, we are happy to stay like this, to return to this. Why change, why diversify, why evolve? It will only bring you sorrow, want and need, cruelty, and you will destroy yourselves and all that has come before you, and we will go back and be us, and we will be all the earth again, we never change, we are one. You may think that life evolved, but it shook us again and again until you occurred, you who are destroying all for yourselves, and we watch you.

I hear the noise of the tea trolley coming, it is rising, trembling, it is like a tsunami, a rehearsal for when the water comes, trembling and filling up the corridor and washing me back to them. The seas are rising, the water is coming to take me back to them, to the quiet, to the dark, and we'll lie curled up in the dark together. And it will start again.

They protested against 24-hour shopping and lights, but I know now that they are all an attempt to return to the bottom of the sea, where endless darkness and 24-hour feeding, eating, sleeping and sex were available, all together, all in one, like globalization. We are returning to one, to the Big Bang, so we can implode together, back into that tiny dot that we all came from, and then we'll curl together so tight that we can't breathe, just be, be, in the darkness together again, all fighting, wars, jealousy, over. All just one.

Jamie knew this, and now he is gone. I thought he was waiting for me, but he was waiting for Melody.

The trees try to shush me, shushing in the wind, lulling me back to sleep, back to the darkness. That's why we lock ourselves in concrete blocks at night, designed to keep their voices out. And the sea, we look at it through car windows so we don't have to face it head on, like an angry parent shouting at us to come home.

If we jumped like lemmings into the sea, like refugees trying to swim to Gibraltar, we could end this, go back, all floating on our backs peacefully.

You do not care that fish drown in the air they are left to gulp. This is the other way round. The rain drives you into your homes, your cars, your aeroplanes, to escape it, but you only make it worse. Hippocampus has tricked you into its bidding.

Music won't help me anymore. Music has become like oil, it's working for oil, no longer wood and horse hair, ivory and wood, it's oil and shiny and discs and electricity, sparkling CDs and tapes and computers and more and more technical, easier to find than play, than create, machines will do it, all for you, oil slides into your ears, you cannot hear the birdsong, you do not notice that it is fading and gone, oil has taken the birds, diesel fumes, to manic beats that beat you down like the machines that make it.

O'Hara says he has given up. That we must try electroshock treatment. That we must target Hippocampus, who is at the centre of all this. That we must induce neuron death, that we must enlarge Hippocampus, that we must induce neuron growth. Hippocampus tells him to start.

I flex upwards, restrained by the ties. It flashes and subsides. I shake like Jamie.

Hippocampus says, 'Now will you be quiet?'

Acknowledgements

Many thanks to Ger Burke and Tony O'Dwyer of
Wordsonthestreet for publishing *Marina*;
to Sarah Clancy, Elaine Feeney, Mike McCormack,
Declan Meade, Alan McMonagle, Danielle McLaughlin
and Conor Montague for encouragement and support;
to Des, Anne and Marie McCann for a childhood full of
books; to Anthony Callanan for love and support and to
Saoirse McCann-Callanan for love and proofreading.